S0-AXO-626

Laura's Luck

by

Marilyn Sachs

AN
APPLE®
PAPERBACK

SCHOLASTIC INC.
New York Toronto London Auckland Sydney Tokyo

To my sister, Jeannie

No part of this publication may be reproduced in whole or in part, or stored in a retrieval system, or transmitted in any form or by any means, electronic, mechanical, photocopying, recording, or otherwise, without written permission of the publisher. For information regarding permission, write to Doubleday & Co., Inc., 245 Park Avenue, New York, NY 10017.

ISBN 0-590-33299-6

Copyright © 1965 by Marilyn Sachs. All rights reserved. Published by Scholastic Inc., 730 Broadway, New York, NY 10003, by arrangement with Doubleday & Co., Inc.

12 11 10 9 8 7 6 5 4 3 2   4 5 6 7 8 9/8

Printed in the U.S.A.   11

**Other APPLE® PAPERBACKS
you will enjoy:**

Amy and Laura
   by Marilyn Sachs
Amy Moves In
   by Marilyn Sachs
Bummer Summer
   by Ann M. Martin
The Door In The Wall
   by Marguerite de Angeli
Just Plain Cat
   by Nancy K. Robinson
Tough-Luck Karen
   by Johanna Hurwitz
Yours Till Niagara Falls, Abby
   by Jane O'Connor

Contents

Off to Camp

When the bus pulled away, Daddy ran alongside of it, calling, "Good-by, good-by . . . don't forget to write." Laura could hear his voice quite clearly but she turned her face away from the window and pretended not to see him.

"Good-by, Daddy, good-by," Amy was shouting and waving.

Just as the bus started to turn the corner, Laura suddenly wanted to see Daddy, wave to him, and throw him a kiss. She stood up, craning her head at the window, but it was too late. The bus had turned.

"Gee," said Amy, "Daddy looked like he was going to cry."

1

Laura flopped back into her seat and nearly began crying herself. She had made Daddy miserable, that's what she'd done. As if he didn't have enough troubles, she'd just gone and made it worse. Why, she was acting like a spoiled, selfish brat — as bad as — yes — as bad as Amy. And if Amy weren't sitting there beside her, she just knew she'd be blubbering all over the place. She took a deep breath, gulped back that persistent lump in her throat, and ran her tongue around the inside of her mouth. And, on top of everything else, her braces were annoying her. After three weeks, you'd think a person would be used to them, but they still felt as if she were carrying a hardware store around inside her mouth. Of course, she wanted pretty, straight teeth, but why couldn't the dentist have waited until after the summer? After all, they'd waited nearly twelve years anyway. Another few months certainly wasn't going to hurt.

"I have no luck," she said out loud.

"What's that?" said Amy.

Laura looked at her sister's even, white teeth smiling at her, and said irritably, "I wasn't talking to you."

2

"Who were you talking to?" Amy's blue eyes looked around questioningly.

"And then she has all those curls too," Laura thought grimly. "Look — just leave me alone," she hissed. "I'm thinking."

"Who's stopping you?" Amy shrugged her shoulders and began opening the paper bag on her lap. She fished out a sandwich and began munching.

"What are you doing?" Laura demanded.

"I'm hungry," said Amy.

"But it's early in the morning. That's supposed to be for lunch."

"But I'm hungry. I was too excited to eat breakfast. This is good. Do you want a bite?"

"No, I don't. And later on, don't think you're going to eat my lunch. Can't you ever do anything right?"

Amy's eyes filled with tears. "You're so mean, Laura," she cried. "Why are you picking on me? What did I do to you?"

"Stop crying!" Laura whispered, glancing around at the bus full of children. "Everybody'll see you."

Amy nodded, took another bite of her sandwich, and chewed away at it while some leftover tears flowed down her face.

"I just hope they put you at one end of camp and me at the other," said Laura consolingly.

Amy burst into loud, wet weeping. Suddenly the bus became very quiet as all the children turned in their direction. Miss Jean, one of the counselors who was traveling with them, worked her way over to their seat.

"What's the matter, honey?" she said in a loud, cheerful voice. "Are you seasick?"

Everybody laughed except Laura. Amy stopped crying and took another bite of her sandwich.

"What's your name?" smiled Miss Jean.

"Amy Stern," Amy said, smiling a little in return.

"How old are you?"

"Ten."

"Good. That means you'll be in my bunk at camp. Come sit over here with me and let's get acquainted."

Clutching her lunch bag, and smiling a big, wide, straight smile, Amy slid past Laura into the encircling arm of Miss Jean, who guided her gently toward the front of the bus. The counselor hadn't even glanced at Laura.

4

"She always has all the luck," Laura thought angrily to herself, that brat! Everybody always takes her part because she's so short and skinny. It doesn't make sense. If she was tall like me, everybody would think she was wrong. Just for one day, let her be me. She'd see what it was like to be the older one, and have a brat for a kid sister. She wouldn't like it one bit.

Memories of past kindnesses on her part flooded her mind. All the maps she'd drawn for Amy for school, all the stories she'd told her, the battles she'd fought for her — the little coward! And what had Amy given her in return? Thanks, respect — hah! Laura reviewed savagely the many examples of betrayal on Amy's part. All the times Amy had taunted her, saying "Buck Teeth!" the way she always tattled, and, worst of all, there was cousin Gladys' party. Well, she'd never forget that. That particular memory was nearly two years old but Laura had nourished it with anguish until it had assumed the proportion of chief outrage in her life.

Parties had always been difficult for Laura. Of course she enjoyed the refreshments and the party decorations, but the agony of standing up before the group to recite a poem or sing a song, as all the guests were expected to do, reduced the pleasure considerably. But Mama always insisted. She was just as good as anybody else, said Mama, and it would help her develop poise.

Well, Laura doubted that very much. However, for cousin Gladys' party, Laura had chosen a very special poem to recite, so very special that she felt she was the only one who could speak the lines as she felt the poet had wanted them spoken. It was about a dead boy, and Laura worked hard developing a low, mournful quality in her voice. She believed firmly that when she finished reciting this poem, all the guests would be in tears. She found herself almost looking forward to reciting.

Amy, who loved performing before groups — anywhere, any size — had been practicing "Don't" by Edgar A. Guest. They recited their poems to one another until they knew them by heart.

The day of the party, Amy got up to recite first. She finished her poem without a slip, and while Laura composed herself, and wondered if everybody could hear her heart beating, Amy looked slyly over toward her and started reciting:

"THE LAMB *by Rachel Field*

Jonathan Preble, agéd three,
Has a lamb for company,
Carved of marble smooth and white
Lest he should be afraid at night
Or lonely by himself all day
Among the other tombstones gray . . ."

Her poem! Her beautiful, wonderful, special poem! On and on, Amy went, reciting the entire poem. She knew the words from beginning to end but she said them all wrong as if it was just a funny jingle. Everybody laughed when she finished. That made it even worse.

Naturally, Mama had scolded Amy, and Daddy had shaken his head (although there was a smile on his face), but Laura would never forget it as long as she lived.

Grumbling to herself, she glanced over to where Amy sat, smiling up at Miss Jean. The brat! Even Mama usually took her part for the completely illogical reason that "she's smaller than you."

Mama. She ran her tongue around the inside of her mouth again. They were still there — and Mama hadn't even seen them. She didn't know when she had felt so miserable in all her life. She pressed her face against the window because in spite of herself there were tears oozing out from the corners of her eyes. Quickly she wiped her hand across her face. She wasn't going to let anybody see *her* cry!

She put her hand in the pocket of her jacket, and pulled out Mama's letter to her. Just seeing it made Laura feel better. It was the first letter that Mama had been able to write since the accident. Only last night, Daddy had brought it home from the hospital. Laura opened it and began reading. Mama's handwriting looked so funny.

July 4

Dearest Laura,

This letter is for you. Kiss Amy, and tell her that the next letter I write will be for her. Laura darling, I know that you're not happy about going to camp and I wish that you didn't have to go since you feel so strongly about it. But there is just no other way. The doctor won't let me come home until after the summer, and you and Amy are too young to look after yourselves. Aunt Minnie needs a vacation. I know you and Amy have done all you could to help her, and she herself has told me over and over again what sweet, good girls you both are. But you must remember, Laura, that Aunt Minnie is not used to taking care of children. She has been with you since December, and needs a rest, I'm sure.

I have a feeling though that you'll enjoy camp very much. Just give it a chance. You're always such a good sport that I know I don't have to remind you how to behave. I worry more about Amy than I do about you. Thank goodness, you are always so dependable. Take care of your little sister. Write soon, and have a very, very good time. I'm so happy to be able to write to you.

All my love,
Mother

Laura folded the letter carefully and put it back in her pocket. "Some good sport I am!" she thought.

Laura and Mama both rated good sportsmanship high on their code of ethics. But ever since Mama had been in the hospital, there were times when Laura's standards had been forgotten. The whole episode over camp, for instance — the way she hadn't spoken to Daddy for two solid days. Now really, what was the point of that! Here Mama's been in the hospital for nearly seven months, Laura thought to herself, and Daddy says she never, not once, complained to him.

She straightened herself up, took a deep breath, and looked bravely around her. Ugh! All she saw was a load of noisy children on their way to camp. And she, amazingly enough, one of them. Feeling more and more like Joan of Arc, Laura moved closer to the window, recognized Alexander's Department Store on Grand Concourse as the bus whizzed by, and started rearranging the accident.

This time Amy was the one who had been hurt, and lay white and unconscious in the ambulance that screamed its way to the hospital. No, no, that wouldn't do! Sooner or later, Laura always felt uneasy when she made it Amy, so she changed it around and put herself, bleeding and unconscious in the hospital stretcher that was wheeled swiftly into the operating room. Sometimes she made it Daddy, sometimes even Aunt Minnie, but sooner or later, she had to return to the real way it happened.

So many times had she thought about that day — over and over again — that every single small detail fell into place with complete precision. She was wearing her navy blue sweater with the moth hole on the left sleeve. Her pen had dripped ink all over her right hand. And the snow lay hard and slippery on the streets. She could remember how icicles formed in her nose as she breathed the freezing air on the way home from school. She hadn't even been thinking about Mama as she opened the door of the apartment. There was a cocoa smell inside that seemed proper and reasonable what with the ice cold outside. But Aunt Minnie, Daddy's older sister, who was a widow, stood there in the kitchen, smiling and looking uncomfortable.

The funny thing was that in her imagination, Laura could see Daddy or Amy, or herself being hit by a skidding car. Clearest of all, she could see Aunt Minnie. But it was impossible seeing it happening to Mama. Well — it was all over now. After the summer, Mama would be home. She should be grateful for that much, she supposed. At first, they weren't even sure Mama would ever come home.

Then, Laura thought grimly, there was Aunt Minnie. She had her good points, of course, but the complete lack of responsibility on her part just floored Laura. At first, when Daddy said Aunt Minnie was coming to stay with them, Laura had been opposed to having her. Why, Mama would be home soon, wouldn't she? What was the point? They could manage by themselves for the short time that Mama would be hospitalized.

But Aunt Minnie came. And the months passed. And Aunt Minnie stayed. And the clanging and banging and crashing that followed in her wake. Why, there just wasn't a quiet spot anywhere in the house for a person who was used to privacy. For Amy, it didn't seem to matter since she spent most of her time outside with her friends. But Laura was used to quiet afternoons, reading, doing her homework, and holding leisurely, rational conversations with Mama.

Aunt Minnie's chief object in life was housecleaning, and apparently she regarded

Laura somewhat as a scout who always sat down in spots that required cleaning. If Laura sat on the couch in the living room, Aunt Minnie dusted the furniture around her. If Laura tried to read in the kitchen, Aunt Minnie needed to wash the kitchen floor. Even if Laura retired into the bedroom she and Amy shared, Aunt Minnie was certain to change the linens. She had explained kindly to Aunt Minnie many times in the beginning how important it was for her to have peace and quiet while she read or did her homework. But Aunt Minnie always said she should go out and play, and that fresh air was good for her.

Then she complained to Daddy but he just laughed. Daddy laughed at the strangest things. He never took anything seriously.

"It's not natural for a child to sit around so much with her nose in a book," she heard Aunt Minnie tell Daddy one night.

Of course Daddy laughed. "She's the smart one in the family," he said. "The bookworm. She's serious, like Hannah. Not like me."

"What do you mean, smart like Hannah?" retorted Aunt Minnie, who had quite a bit of family pride. "There's nothing wrong with your head, Harry. And a little fun never hurt anybody."

In the end, Laura arranged a compromise with Aunt Minnie. A few days a week, she went over to Sally Robinson's house to study, or she went to the library, and on the days that she stayed home, Aunt Minnie tried her best to confine her housekeeping activities to adjacent rooms.

They had developed a satisfactory working arrangement, and Laura had even accepted Aunt Minnie's presence as inevitable until Mama returned from the hospital. Then, without warning, Aunt Minnie announced that she needed a rest, and was going to visit Aunt Sophie in Albany for the summer. Daddy said fine, Mama from the hospital said fine, and they both decided the girls would enjoy going to camp.

Maybe Amy would enjoy going to camp, but couldn't they see how ridiculous it was for her to go to camp? Even Mama — darling Mama — who always understood these matters, seemed so thoughtless.

Reluctantly, Laura glanced around the bus once more, and listened distastefully to the shrill, excited voices. "A good sport," "dependable." That's what Mama had written. Laura winced. Well, it wouldn't be easy but she'd try.

She glanced guiltily over at Amy, who was now working her way down a large banana and talking at the same time to Miss Jean. How small her face looked behind that banana. And suddenly she felt very tender about Amy.

"Poor little kid," she thought. "It's been hard for her too. She's the one who's being a good sport, not me. I'll make it up to her though. From now on, I'll just stop acting like a baby."

She kept looking at Amy, trying to catch her eye. But Amy was all wrapped up in her banana. Laura stared as hard as she could at Amy, and finally Amy looked up, right at her. Laura smiled her sweetest, widest smile, not even caring if her braces did show. What else could she do to show Amy she was sorry? Oh yes! She held up her bag of lunch, pointed to it, and then to Amy.

Her sister's forehead wrinkled in surprise. But in a moment, she smiled and nodded.

Well now, that was settled. Laura leaned back in her seat and looked out of the win-

dow. There was something else she had to
do. What was it? Oh yes — Daddy. In the
other pocket of her jacket was a postcard
that Daddy had addressed to himself, and
that she was to mail as soon as they arrived
in camp. Daddy had even written a message
to himself on the other side. It said:

Dear Daddy,
    We arrived safely and we didn't lose
anything.
                            Love and kisses,
                            Laura and Amy

"Do you have a pencil I could borrow?"
she asked the girls seated behind her. They
did not.

She leaned forward and tapped the girl's
shoulder in front of her. "Do you have a
pencil I could borrow?" Yes, the girl did.

There was quite a bit of space left under
the message Daddy had written on the postcard. Laura wrote:

Dear Daddy,
    I waved to you after the bus started.
but you didn't see me. I'm sorry I was
such a pill. Don't worry about us. We'll

be fine. Have a nice summer. Lots of love from —

> Your affectionate daughter,
> Laura

There. That did it. She would write him a letter tomorrow or the next day telling him some pleasant things about camp. There was bound to be something pleasant she could tell him. An unhappy feeling spread all over her again. She just didn't want to go to camp.

"That's enough of that!" she said to herself sharply. "No sense crying over spilt milk. Be a good sport now."

She leaned over again, and tapped the girl's shoulder. "Here's your pencil. Thanks a lot."

"You're welcome." The girl turned around and smiled at Laura. They both waited for a moment, looking at each other.

"She looks smart," Laura noted approvingly as she finally dropped her eyes. She wished she could think of something to say.

"My name is Anne Sherman," the girl began. "What's your name?"

"Laura Stern."

"I'm twelve and a half. How old are you?"

"I'll be twelve August 11th."

"I'm in 7B."

"So am I."

"How come?"

"I skipped."

"Oh."

There was a pause while each girl took a deep breath.

"Was that your sister crying like that?" began Anne on the second round.

"Yes."

"Why was she crying?"

Laura was silent.

"What's her name?"

"Amy."

"How old is she?"

"Ten."

"I have a sister too."

Now it was Laura's turn. "What's her name?"

"Paula."

"How old is she?"

"Eleven last week."

"Where is she?"

Anne made a face, and motioned toward the head next to her. Both girls laughed.

"Can I come and sit next to you for a while?" asked Anne.

"Oh, yes," said Laura.

Anne got up and moved over beside Laura. They spent another quiet moment looking each other over. Both girls had straight brown hair and brown eyes, and both were tall.

"We look alike," thought Laura.

"You know, we look alike," said Anne, giggling.

Ordinarily, Laura held a low opinion of girls who giggled. It seemed to go along with poor grades in school and an interest in boys. She regarded Anne just a little suspiciously for a moment, but hearing no further danger signs, decided to overlook it.

Some children in the back began singing. Soon others joined in.

"Skin-a-ma-rink-a-dink-a-dink
Skin-a-ma-rink-a-do
Camp Tiorati we love you
Skin-a-ma-rink-a-dink-a-dink
Skin-a-ma-rink-a-do
Camp Tiorati — we'll be true.

We love you in the morning
And we love you in the night
We love you when we're far away
And you are out of sight
Oh — Skin-a-ma-rink-a-dink-a-dink
Skin-a-ma-rink-a-do
We'll be true!"

"Isn't it exciting?" shouted Anne over the noise. "Did you ever go to camp before? This is my first time."

"Me too."

"We certainly have a lot of things in common," yelled Anne. "Is your sister a brat?"

"Only sometimes," said Laura loyally.

"Mine is all the time," said Anne.

But the singing had grown too loud for conversation. Soon Anne had joined in, and even Laura found herself humming along in a monotone.

"Dum, dum, dum, dum," they sang as the bus made its way out of the city, across the bridge, and into the country.

After a while, the singing gave way to the rustling of paper bags as more and more children discovered they were starving. Amy returned to collect her share of Laura's lunch, and Anne got up to return to her own seat.

"I guess we'll be in the same bunk in camp," she said. "Let's try to get beds next to each other."

"OK," Laura said, very pleased.

"Let's eat," said Amy, sliding back into her seat. Her thin, little face was beaming. "Miss Jean is so nice," she told Laura. "I'm glad she's going to be my counselor. You know she said we'd be going on overnight camping trips, and we'd have a campfire every night, and roast hot dogs, and marshmallows. Gee, I'm hungry."

Laura patted her sister's arm affectionately.

"You can have half my lunch," she said.

"Thanks, Laura. I'm glad you're not grouchy any more. I told Miss Jean that you weren't mean all the time, and that sometimes you could even be very nice."

"Thanks," Laura said sharply. She opened her bag of lunch and was astonished at all the things Aunt Minnie had stashed away inside. There were two chicken sandwiches, two hard-boiled eggs, some carrot sticks, a banana, a peach, two plums, and four chocolate sandwich cookies.

"Did you eat all your lunch?" she asked in surprise.

"No," Amy said indignantly, "I gave one of the cookies to a girl named Patty."

For a while the bus driver enjoyed almost complete peace and quiet as the contents of numerous paper bags were ravenously dispatched. However, as soon as the fueling-up process had been completed, the singing began once more.

"Oh you can't get to heaven," sang one
    group of children.
"Oh you can't get to heaven," answered
    another.

"On roller skates."
"On roller skates."

"Cause you'll roll right by."
"Cause you'll roll right by."

"Those Pearly Gates."
"Those Pearly Gates."

"Oh you can't get to heaven," sang every-
    body together,
"On roller skates
Cause you'll roll right by those Pearly Gates.
I ain't gonna grieve my Lord no more.

22

I ain't gonna grieve my Lord no more,
I ain't gonna grieve my Lord no more,
I ain't gonna grie — eve my Lord no more."

"I think it's going to be wonderful," said
Amy, brushing the last crumbs off her lap.
"I hope so," said Laura.

Welcome to Camp Tiorati

"The Indians," Miss Partridge continued, "not so long ago, sat in the very same spot where all of you are seated today. They fished and swam in the waters of Lake Tiorati where you too will fish and swim. They roamed through the same forest that surrounds us now."

She smiled encouragingly at the girls seated on the grass. "They did not," she said, her voice rising, "enjoy the so-called wonders of civilization. But the wonders of nature were theirs."

Laura scratched a brand-new mosquito bite, and looked around her indulgently. So this was camp. There seemed to be lots of trees with real, old-fashioned log cabins peeping out from behind them. Miss Partridge, the director, had just explained to them triumphantly that there were very few city comforts in Camp Tiorati so that the girls would be able to enjoy nature all the more. Laura really could not see the connection between hot and cold running water and enjoying nature but Miss Partridge seemed to feel very strongly about it.

She also wondered a little at Miss Partridge's appearance. First of all she seemed very old — maybe even as old as Grandma — tiny too, with a pointed little face like a bird's. But the most surprising thing of all was the way she dressed. She wore a huge sun hat, a bright pink shirt, and — amazingly enough — blue jeans and sneakers. In all her life, Laura had never seen an old lady who wore jeans. She doubted whether Mama or Aunt Minnie would approve.

"Many things," Miss Partridge was saying, "will seem strange at first to those of you who have never been to camp before. But very soon, I know, you will forget about your city comforts. There are so many new and lovely things in store for you — so many wonders for you to discover. I hope each of you will feel when camp is over that this has been a summer to remember. And now, your counselors are waiting to show you to your bunks. Let me welcome you again to Camp Tiorati. In the words of our song, 'We're mighty glad you're here.' "

The girls applauded, a few even cheered. A little quiver of excitement flowed through the group. Now that the welcoming speech was over, the real business of finding out about camp would begin. Laura looked nervously over at Amy. They would certainly be separated — for the first time in their lives. At home they shared the same room, and even the same bed. Would Amy be upset? But Amy was happily chattering with some girls in back of her. Laura licked her braces reflectively. Perhaps Amy wouldn't mind being separated from her. For a moment she felt hurt and very lonely. People generally liked Amy and she seldom seemed to feel shy or awkward the way Laura did. She's lucky that way, thought Laura.

There were three very strong feelings that Laura had in connection with Amy. The first was annoyance, which she felt most of the time. The second was protection, which involved Laura, who never fought on her own account, in numerous scuffles since Amy could never fight her own battles. And the third — which Laura was very careful never to reveal to her younger sister — was pride. It was this last feeling that Laura began feeling at this moment.

"She'll be all right, my sister," she thought admiringly. "I won't have to worry about her."

"I wonder which one is going to be our counselor," said Anne, who sat next to her.

Laura nodded absently, and thought to herself, "If she's twelve and a half, and only in 7B, that means she never skipped." Still, marks didn't always mean everything. Joan Borkowski, in her class in school, never got high grades but she did play the violin beautifully, and was an intelligent, serious girl. She looked tolerantly at Anne. Maybe she's interested in music. There hadn't been much opportunity to talk on the bus but with the whole summer ahead of them they'd have plenty of time to compare notes. Laura began to feel lighter inside. Imagine — she'd made a friend without even trying.

Miss Partridge began speaking again. She introduced all the smiling counselors to the group. "Now," she said, "will all the eight-year-olds come over to Miss Harriet. She will be your counselor, and will take you to your bunk. All the nine-year-olds come over to Miss Gladys, the ten-year-olds to Miss Jean, the eleven-year-olds to Miss Sandra, the twelve-year-olds to Miss Susan, and the thirteen-year-olds to Miss Carol."

Laura sat still while all around her the children jumped to their feet and hurried off to meet their new counselors.

"I'll see you later," Amy called back over her shoulder.

"Come on," said Anne, "let's go!"

"But what should I do?" Laura said, slowly rising. "I'm still eleven even though I'll be twelve in a few weeks."

"Oh, don't worry about that," Anne said impatiently. "You're practically twelve, and besides you're in 7B, aren't you?"

"I guess so," Laura said thoughtfully. "Maybe I should tell the counselor though."

"You can if you want to but I don't think it matters. Come on, let's go."

Miss Susan was already surrounded by a chattering bunch of girls when they arrived. "Two more candidates," she said smiling. "My, we're going to be a large group."

Laura cleared her throat. She supposed Anne was right and there was no point in mentioning all the details about her age but she just wouldn't feel right unless Miss Susan knew.

"Miss Susan," she said quickly, "I'm not really twelve yet but I will be in a few . . ."

"What was that, honey?" asked the counselor.

"I'm not really twelve yet," said Laura, uncomfortably, "but I will be in a few weeks."

"Well then, you'll still have to go along with Miss Sandra's group," said Miss Susan cheerfully.

"But she's nearly twelve," cried Anne, hurrying to her defense, "and besides, she's in 7B, same as me."

Laura looked gratefully at Anne. She was not used to having somebody protect her. It was a sweet feeling.

"That makes no difference," continued Miss Susan, still smiling. "A rule is a rule. If we break it for her, lots of other girls who are nearly one age or another would feel it wasn't fair. You can understand that, can't you, honey?"

Laura nodded miserably. The terrible thing was that she could understand it.

Lying in her bed that night, Laura tried desperately to push back those horrible feelings of homesickness that kept crowding into her head. There had been enough weeping and wailing in her bunk for one night. Paula, Anne's younger sister, who slept in the bed next to hers, had been particularly difficult. But right now it sounded as if she must have sniffed herself to sleep at long last.

Everybody was quiet now. Long ago, it seemed, the last forlorn notes of taps had died away. Through the screened windows unfamiliar country noises pressed in. Crickets, she supposed — maybe the wind pushing around the branches of the big pine trees that seemed to be everywhere. She could feel cool air blowing on her face, and eased herself down into the small, tight bed.

Funny how cool it became at night in the country. In the city now, she knew, it would be too hot to sleep. Everybody — grownups and children too — would be out on the street, sitting on the stoops, sucking lemon or raspberry ices, and talking and laughing to each other. Sometimes Daddy would take them over to the candy store for chocolate egg creams. Usually they could stay up as late as they wanted.

"Now you be a good sport!" she whispered fiercely to herself, feeling an uncontrollable wave of homesickness. "You're not going to like it here, that's obvious, but nobody has to know."

Tonight she had been too miserable, but tomorrow she would write cheerful letters to Daddy and Mama. Oh, she could tell them all about the lake, and the beautiful trees — describe the scenery — that's right. Grownups always seemed to be interested in scenery. Then — well, she couldn't lie and say she was having a good time but then she needn't say anything about herself at all. She'd just tell them about Amy. That, at least, was one thing she didn't have to worry about. Amy was happy, and not at all homesick. She had spoken to Amy while they were getting ready for bed — trudging, it seemed endlessly to her, from their bunks to the outdoor cold-water washing stands, to the latrines off on a little hill, and back again. Amy had separated herself from her bunkmates and hurried over to Laura somewhere along that long march.

Her eyes were shining. "It's wonderful," she said ecstatically. "I just love it. I'm so glad we came. Aren't you?"

Laura avoided a direct answer. "I'm glad you're having such a good time," she said.

"Where's Anne?" Amy asked, looking around for her.

"Oh, we're in different bunks," Laura said, trying miserably to sound indifferent.

But Amy was too involved in her own pleasure to notice that something was wrong, and she soon dashed away to join her group.

"She's fine anyway," Laura thought gratefully. "I can write most of my letters about her." As for herself — better avoid mentioning anything at all. After all, what was there to say? That she had been separated from Anne? That she was in a bunk with a bunch of eleven-year-old babies? And that her counselor didn't like her?

Of course she realized with justice that Miss Sandra was trying very hard to be fair. But you can always tell when grown-ups don't like you. They act fair. Miss Sandra had smiled at her, and called her by her name certainly as many times if not more than any of the other girls in the group. She had even put an arm around Laura's shoulder walking back from the mess hall this evening. But she had put her hands over her ears while Paula was chattering to her and said, "Cut it out! You're driving me crazy!" and she had shaken her head ruefully over the way little blond Adrienne had fumbled with hospital corners, and said, "You're impossible." She liked them. But to Laura, she was fair and polite.

"I can't blame her," Laura thought sadly. "I've been such a sourpuss." But how in the world could she possibly warm up to the girls in her bunk when Anne was the only friend she wanted? And besides, these girls were children — most of them in 6A or 6B. Only one other girl was in the 7th, and then only in 7A. It was humiliating. All day long, she had hung back, lagged behind, sat a little distance away from them. The others thought she was stuck-up, and only Paula continued, maddeningly, to chatter away to her.

She knew Miss Sandra was watching her, and trying to draw her into the group. Miss Sandra did not seem to understand how great was the distance between eleven and practically twelve.

"What would you like to do tonight after supper, Laura?" she asked while the girls were discussing their plans.

"I don't care," she had replied, noting the disappointment on Miss Sandra's face.

Or — "Laura, you look as if you'd be good at volleyball. You're so tall."

"I don't like sports," she had answered truthfully.

Laura flopped over on her stomach and buried her face in the pillow. "I'm just not being a good sport," she said again, "but tomorrow I'll really try. After all, it's only for eight weeks, and what," she nearly groaned out loud, "is eight weeks? It'll just fly by."

Much later, Laura woke up because something wet had fallen on her face, and something was shaking her shoulder. It was dark but she knew immediately that Amy stood there by her bed crying.

"Whatsamatter?" she said sleepily.

"Oh, Laura, I'm so homesick and lonely," wailed Amy.

"Shh, shh," Laura whispered, "you'll wake everybody up."

Amy continued sobbing but an octave

lower. "Please, can I come in bed with you? I'm so lonely in my bed." More sobs.

"All right," Laura said sympathetically. And when Amy had snuggled under her covers, both girls hugged each other, and contentedly drifted back to sleep.

The next time she woke up, a flashlight was shining in her face.

"Here she is," someone said in a relieved tone.

Miss Jean and Miss Sandra, both in bathrobes, stood by her bed, looking very large.

"Come on, Amy," said Miss Jean, gently shaking her, "let's go back to bed."

"No," moaned Amy, "I want to stay here."

"Come on now," Miss Jean continued, trying to help Amy up. But Amy threw her arms around Laura's neck and began sobbing, "I want to stay here. I want to go home. I want Mama."

Laura held her sister as tight as she could, and snapped at her tormentors, "Leave her alone! Go away!" She was still very sleepy but even so, there was something familiar about all this. It happened all the time. Somebody was bothering her little sister and only she could protect her.

"Stop it, Laura!" Miss Sandra said in exasperation. "You'll wake everybody up. Let go of her this instant."

But then Miss Jean kneeled by the bed and patted Amy's shoulder affectionately. "Come on, sweetheart. Come with Miss Jean, and let's all get back to sleep. Come on, darling."

The kindness in her voice was irresistible. Slowly, Amy withdrew her arms from around Laura's neck, took Miss Jean's hand, and walked off with her.

Fully awake now, and feeling very foolish, Laura looked up into the unfriendly face of her own counselor. But when Miss Sandra spoke, her voice was polite and reasonable again.

"You're older than she is," she said. "You should have known better. Now go to sleep please."

She hurried off after Miss Jean, and Laura could hear her say, "I guess there's always one in every group."

Laura lay down again, missing Amy terribly.

"I have no luck," she said.

A Good Sport

"Arts and Crafts this morning," Miss Sandra said briskly. Laura looked longingly at the books on the orange crate by the side of her bed. Each girl had an orange crate in which she could keep things like soap, toothbrush, towel, and various other items for handy reference. For her summer reading, Laura had brought three books she'd been anxious to read for some time. They were *David Copperfield* by Charles Dickens, *Arrowsmith* by Sinclair Lewis, and *Matorni's Vineyard* by E. Phillips Oppenheim. The first two had been recommended by her teacher last term, and the third was part of a set of books that Mama had bought before she was married. Laura thought she would like to read *Matorni's Vineyard* first and then go on to the others. Not far from their cabin was a huge tree with a seat built all around its trunk. Laura could think of nothing she'd rather do than spend the morning there reading her book.

But after breakfast they all returned to their bunk to make their beds and tidy up the cabin. Miss Sandra encouraged them in their work by explaining that each morning the bunk that finished first received a flag that was hung over its doorway for all to see. This resulted in lots of speed and giggling on the part of the girls in Laura's bunk but somehow the mysteries of hospital corners were too much for too many of them. They finished next to last, the eight-year-olds being last.

"Tomorrow's another day," said Miss Sandra, trying to sound hopeful.

Next came chores. "This camp belongs to you," Miss Sandra explained, "and it's up to all of you to see that it's kept clean and attractive, and to help in every way you can. Some mornings our bunk will be assigned to KP — helping out in the kitchen.

Other mornings we'll clean the latrines, and so on. Today, we're the sanitation detail. That means that all of you will walk around the grounds picking up paper and anything else that doesn't belong there. When you're finished with that, you will find a small garbage can in front of each bunk. You will have to empty all of those into the large cans in back of the mess hall. Work in pairs and you'll find it easier. Report back here when you're finished. It shouldn't take you more than half an hour."

"Hup, two, three," said Paula, as she and Laura walked out of the bunk together. Paula had attached herself to Laura, who did not appreciate it at all. Really, she had nothing against Paula, except that she was Anne's kid sister and a pest.

She began picking up pieces of paper and half listened to Paula talking about Nancy Drew books. That was another thing; she had nothing against Nancy Drew books either, but she had finished reading every single one of them over a year ago.

She worked steadily on, gleaning pieces of paper and steeling herself in her resolve to be a good sport. Miss Sandra certainly had been very nice this morning, not saying a word to her about last night. There were fresh mosquito bites on Laura's face and arms and in between collecting papers she scratched vigorously. The screened window just over her bed had a sizeable hole in it but, after all, that was such a small thing she certainly wasn't going to mention it to Miss Sandra. It was the least she could do to show her counselor that she appreciated her not mentioning the scene over Amy. What were a few mosquito bites anyway!

After chores the girls reassembled in their bunk, and heard about Arts and Crafts. Well — she'd have plenty of chances, she guessed, to read *Matorni's Vineyard*, and besides, there *were* some things she'd like to make for Mama and Daddy, and maybe even Aunt Minnie. Certainly it would be nice to come home from camp with beautiful gifts that she had made herself.

The Arts and Crafts shack was a cabin, just like the one they slept in, but it was filled with baskets, Indian-type blankets hanging on the walls, and large pots of flowers in different corners of the room. Miss Rosalie, the Arts and Crafts counselor, was busy throwing big hunks of clay down on a table as they came in. Pam — she threw the clay down hard, picked it up again, pam — threw it down again, picked it up again, pam. . . .

"Come in, girls," she said, "I'll be with you in a moment."

A few more pams, and then Miss Rosalie seemed satisfied. She turned to the girls and began speaking to them. Like most of the other counselors, she wore jeans and sneakers. But around her neck hung a curious necklace.

"We try here," she said, "to make not only beautiful things, but also to use the materials that are all around us."

She waved one hand in the direction of the baskets and said, "These are made from reeds that grow around the lake. We go out and pick them ourselves."

"Pottery," she said, handling the clay again, and giving it another pam, "we make from clay that we dig out of clay beds close by.

"And wait 'til you see this," she continued proudly, pulling out a basket from under a table. She fished around inside it and held up two dark red woven belts with fringes at the ends. "Not only were these woven on handmade looms that we make here but we also dyed them ourselves from red sumac berries."

She pulled another belt out of the basket, yellow this time, and said triumphantly, "You'll never guess what gave us this lovely color!"

The girls couldn't guess.

Miss Rosalie waited a few minutes before telling them.

"Onions," she said finally, and laughed heartily when she saw the surprise on most of their faces.

"Yes, ordinary onions," she elaborated, and went on to explain to the group that the Indians, with patience and imagination, used the gifts that nature offered them to fashion crafts of great beauty.

"We try to do the same," she said, and then asked if there were any girls who had any particular ideas in mind.

"I do," said Laura, inspired by Miss Rosalie's words, and eager to get to work at once. "I'd like to make a wallet."

Smiling patiently, Miss Rosalie said gently, "Leathercraft is not exactly what I would consider making use of the materials around us. The Indians, of course, did not have wallets. Naturally, they did use leather for moccasins and other items of clothing but then they used the skins of animals they had hunted. Some camps, I suppose, do have the facilities to teach campers how to skin animals and prepare the hide, but" — Miss Rosalie's voice drifted off dreamily — "we don't do anything like that here, unfortunately. Why don't you look around and I'm sure you'll get some other ideas."

Quickly Laura agreed. She was beginning to feel, for the first time in her life, somewhat impatient with the Indians.

While looking at some of the brightly colored, strangely shaped pots that were exhibited in different parts of the shack, Laura suddenly thought of something wonderful for Mama. Aunt Rhoda had a marble candy dish with three birds perched on the rim. Mama always admired that dish and so why didn't she make a dish like that — out of clay, of course.

"I think I'd like to make a — a — bowl," Laura said, next time Miss Rosalie came in her direction. She had nearly said candy dish when she knew very well that Indians didn't have candy dishes.

"Fine," beamed Miss Rosalie.

She proceeded to show Laura how to

build up a bowl by the "coil method." This consisted of rolling out long, snakelike strips of clay, and placing them one on top of the other until the desired height of the bowl was reached. The coils were then smoothed out, and the bowl, after drying for a few days, was ready for glazing and firing.

When Laura rolled out coils they were not at all as smooth as Miss Rosalie's had been. Nevertheless, she worked away patiently until under her hands stood a low, widemouthed bowl. True, there was a bump on one side that could not be smoothed down, and the rim did not seem to be the same height all the way around but Laura was pleased. When she got the birds on it, then it would really look like something. She picked up a small piece of clay, twisted it around in her fingers, and found with amazement a beautiful bird, wings outstretched, lying in the palm of her hand. Gingerly she fastened it to the rim of her bowl. She picked up another piece of clay. In a minute, another bird with outstretched wings perched on top of the bowl. Deftly she made the third, and then it was all finished. It looked lovely. She could hardly wait for Miss Rosalie to see it, and smiled longingly in her direction.

"Are you finished?" asked Miss Rosalie, and walked over to inspect.

Laura kept her eyes modestly averted as the counselor examined the bowl. She was almost embarrassed by the praise that would certainly be forthcoming.

"Well," said Miss Rosalie slowly, "that's very interesting."

Laura waited.

"Of course," continued Miss Rosalie pleasantly, "the bowl would be much better without the birds."

"You — you — don't like the birds?" asked Laura, astonished.

"Well, aside from aesthetic reasons," Miss Rosalie said, "the birds would be certain to break. You just can't make something like that out of clay — it's too fragile. Besides, designwise, the beauty of the bowl is disturbed by sticking those things up there. It interrupts the purity of the line."

Afraid that Miss Rosalie would bring in the Indians again, Laura quickly nodded and said sadly, "I see." But she didn't really see.

After Miss Rosalie moved away, Laura

removed the birds and laid them carefully on their backs on the table. Poor little things, she thought lovingly. Stripped of the birds, the bowl looked to her neither pure nor beautiful — just lopsided. But she placed it on the drying shelf as Miss Rosalie had directed, and was happy when the session ended.

Next came swimming in the clear, very cold waters of Lake Tiorati. Laura floated on her back, and looked up. All she could see was the sky. Between herself and the sky there was nothing — she had it all to herself. Around her, the voices of the other girls sounded far, far away. She was alone with the sky.

The whistle sounded and Laura stood up, searching around for Paula. When they found each other, they joined right hands and raised them high above their heads. The other girls did the same. This was known as the "buddy system," and indicated to the waterfront counselor that all persons who had gone into the water could be accounted for.

As Laura came shivering out of the lake, stumbling a little on the rocks at the bottom, she did think lovingly for one minute about the pool in Crotona Park, back in the city, which had warm water, a tiled floor, and where one could swim and float undisturbed for an entire afternoon. But only for a moment did she allow herself the luxury of such thoughts. She was determined to be a good sport.

Later that afternoon, Miss Sandra suggested a game of volleyball. Most of the girls agreed, and Laura smiled her cooperative smile. Sports as a rule bored her completely. She still hadn't started reading *Matorni's Vineyard* but perhaps tomorrow she'd have a chance.

Miss Sandra placed Laura in the back of her team, since she was so tall. But whenever the ball did come her way, she didn't seem able to do very much with it. One hand, she felt, needed to be free at all times to guard her braces, which left her with only one hand to hit the ball.

"Let yourself go, Laura," urged Miss Sandra. "Jump up and hit the ball with both hands. It's not going to hurt you."

So the next time a ball flew above the heads in front of her, Laura let herself go. High up she jumped, feeling an unfamiliar pleasure in her flight. With both hands she smacked the ball hard, sending it hurtling back over the net, and scoring a point for her team.

"Beautiful!" said Miss Sandra.

But Laura scored no more points for the rest of the game. After hitting the ball, Laura's downward flight was not as pleasant as the upward. She landed hard on her left foot, and felt a sharp pain shooting through her ankle. But once that was over she found she could stand on it without too much discomfort. No point in mentioning it and spoiling the game, she decided, and continued playing but without any more brilliant leaps.

That night they had their first campfire. Sitting there with all the others, Laura enjoyed for the first time the pleasure of being alone. The bright fire roaring in the center and darkness on all their faces. She didn't have to smile. Deep in her warm jacket she was safe against the cold night air, and very comfortable. Most of the girls were singing but in between the voices came the stillness from the forest around them.

As the fire dwindled down, the group rose, and crossing their arms in front of them each girl took the hand of her neighbor to form a friendship ring. Laura sighed — if only camp could always feel like this.

Walking back to her bunk, Laura's ankle seemed much more painful than before. "Probably, it'll be gone by tomorrow," she thought. She was so tired after dragging herself on the now familiar trek to the latrine, the washing stands, and back to her bunk, that gratefully, she eased herself into the tight, little bed.

"Well, it's been a day," she thought as sleep quickly settled down upon her. "But at least I'm being a good sport."

Northern Lights

The next morning Laura's ankle had swollen somewhat but at first it didn't seem terribly painful. She considered mentioning it to Miss Sandra but then decided not to. This wasn't the first time she had sprained her ankle, and she knew from past experience that generally it took only a day or two to mend. Besides, she didn't want to focus any more attention on herself. She just wanted to be an ordinary member of the group.

After chores, Miss Sandra took the girls over to the Nature Shack, where Miss Helen, the nature counselor, spoke to them. There were a few cages and boxes lined up on one side of the shack with nothing inside them. Miss Helen said hopefully that she expected by the end of the summer all the various groups would have collected different kinds of animals for the Nature Shack. She told them about the frogs, salamanders, snakes, and chipmunks that former campers had collected. The girls squealed when she said snakes.

Aside from animals, said Miss Helen, anything else that interested them, like leaves, rocks, or flowers, could be brought to her and she would be very pleased to assist in identifying them. Then Miss Sandra asked them if they would like to take a nature walk that very morning, collecting specimens for the Nature Shack and climbing up to the top of Mt. Kahagon, where they could admire the view and have a cookout lunch. The cookout lunch decided everyone in favor of the project.

In a short while, every girl had a knapsack on her back containing something of the following: hot dogs, buns, apples, maps, compass, rope, matches, first-aid kit, small ax, jackknife, and whistle (to be used only if the bearer found herself separated from the rest of the group). They carried no real cooking equipment since they were going to roast their hot dogs on green sticks over the fire. Some other time, Miss Sandra promised, they would go on an overnight hike and do some real fancy outdoor cooking. In addition to this, each girl carried a metal can in which to collect her nature specimens.

Laura winced as the group began winding up the trail that led to the top of Mt. Kahagon. Maybe she should have said something about her ankle to Miss Sandra but now it was too late. She certainly did not want to spoil everybody's good time. After they came down from the mountain she'd just mention it to her counselor, and then try to stay off her feet for the rest of the day.

For a while the group walked along steadily on the trail. The forest swallowed them up almost as soon as they left the campgrounds. Except for the trail, which was wide enough for only two or three to walk abreast, they were surrounded by tall, silent trees. Under their feet was a carpet of generations of pine needles. It was cool in the forest. Up above, the sky was very blue but only occasionally did the sun manage to shine through the thick, interlocking branches. A person felt very small in all this bigness.

After a while, Miss Sandra began showing them things. She pointed out a little red spot painted on some of the trees which she said marked the way for them. This was known as blazing a trail. The girls began to chatter again. Soon they were singing.

"The bear went over the mountain
The bear went over the mountain
The bear went over the mountain
And what do you think he saw?

He saw another mountain
He saw another mountain
He saw another mountain
And what do you think he did?

He climbed another mountain
He climbed another mountain
He climbed another mountain
And what do you think he saw?

He saw another mountain..."

In between singing and chattering the girls stopped now and then to pick up leaves or rocks and drop them into their cans. Nobody found any snakes although nobody particularly wanted to anyway.

Every time Laura took a step now she felt as if it was absolutely impossible to take another one. They came to a stream finally that was forded by a thick tree trunk over which the girls began crossing, one at a time. Laura was at the end of the line now. After the girl in front of her had scampered across, Laura stood still, licking her braces thoughtfully. There was only one thought in her head at that moment. She knew she could not get across that tree trunk. This was as far as she could go.

"Come on, Laura," called Miss Sandra, "you can do it."

Miserably, Laura shook her head. "I can't do it," she said. Once she had said it, it was true. She sat down on the ground, and the pleasure of getting her weight off that agonizing ankle was so great that she nearly laughed.

Back over the tree trunk came Miss Sandra. "What is it now?" she said just a little irritably. "We'll be there pretty soon."

"My ankle," said Laura, "I sprained it."

Miss Sandra knelt beside her and efficiently pulled Laura's sock down as far as it would go.

"Whew," she said, "you sure did sprain it. Look at that swelling! When did this happen?"

"Yesterday," replied Laura, in a very small voice, "while we were playing volleyball."

"Yesterday!" Miss Sandra repeated blankly. She wrinkled her forehead and looked curiously at Laura.

"If it happened yesterday why didn't you tell me yesterday?"

It was impossible to answer that question sensibly. Laura just shook her head and looked pleadingly at the counselor.

"I just don't understand you, Laura," Miss Sandra said slowly. "Now we'll all have to go back."

Laura hung her head and bit her lip hard. She was so close to crying. There — she had gone and spoiled everybody's good time. Just what she had tried so hard to avoid. What was the matter with her anyway? Couldn't she do anything right? Why did she always have to be different from everybody else?

Miss Sandra patted her shoulder mechanically. Then she got up, called all the girls and told them they would have to go back because Laura had sprained her ankle. She did not mention that Laura had sprained her ankle yesterday. The girls grumbled but came back over the stream and gathered around Laura, looking down at her.

Miss Sandra opened her knapsack and poked around inside. Finally she pulled out a large, white square of material.

"You see now," she told the group, "why you must always bring first-aid supplies along — even on a short hike like this. You can never tell when someone might get hurt."

She looked at Laura, and smiled an encouraging smile. "This will make your ankle feel better, Laura, and when we get back to camp, we'll have the nurse take over."

Briskly she began wrapping the cloth tightly around Laura's ankle, pointing out to the group as she worked the correct way to bind up a sprained ankle.

When she had finished, she helped Laura up and told her to try to walk. Laura did. It was better she supposed but the ankle was still terribly painful. She groaned every time she put her foot down. Miss Sandra thought for a moment. Then she showed Paula how they could make a chair out of their arms for Laura to sit in. She told Laura to put her arms around their necks and to sit down.

Slowly the group began lumbering down the trail. The other girls had to divide the contents of three extra knapsacks between them and they complained. Also, it was getting close to lunchtime and everybody was hungry with no delightful prospect of hot dogs roasting over a fire to look forward to.

After Paula had thought she was stepping on a snake, and pulled up her arms suddenly, causing Laura to fall, Miss Sandra told Ruth to take over as the other half of the human chair. When Ruth's arms grew tired, Adrienne took over. After Adrienne came Wilma.

Very slowly, the group jiggled and joggled its way down the mountain. Nobody talked very much and nobody sang at all. The sun, directly overhead now, blazed down upon them. By the time they finally reached the campgrounds, they were so hot, tired, and hungry that nobody could think of anything else.

"Boy I'm hot!" said Adrienne.

"My arms hurt!" said Wilma.

"When do we eat?" moaned Paula.

Miss Sandra helped Laura sit down on the grass, and with a grateful sigh, began rubbing her arms.

"Well — we made it!" she said.

Laura tried to look grateful. She also tried to look uncomplaining and inconspicuous. Every part of her body ached — but through the discomfort, she could see the unfriendly glances her bunkmates cast in her direction. That was even worse — especially since she deserved it.

"Well, well, well," came a cheerful voice, "it looks like our wanderers have returned."

Laura looked up and saw Miss Partridge, the camp director, smiling down at them. Just for a moment, she wondered, crossly, why people in this camp always had to be so cheerful.

"Laura sprained her ankle," reported Paula, "so we had to come right back."

"And we didn't have our cookout," somebody else added.

"And you're all hungry," laughed Miss Partridge. "I can see that quite plainly."

She and Miss Sandra walked a little distance away from the group and spoke softly to each other. When they returned, Miss

Partridge said, "There's no reason why you still can't have your cookout right here in camp. I can get Laura over to the infirmary myself — it's close by — so the rest of you scoot now, and have a good time."

The girls brightened, and hurried off with Miss Sandra.

"We'll get lunch for you, Laura, right after Miss Frances, the nurse, gets you comfortable," said Miss Partridge, helping Laura up. She had Laura put an arm across her shoulder, put her own arm around Laura's waist, and told her to hop on her good foot. Miss Partridge was tiny but Laura was surprised at her strength. It felt almost as if she were being carried.

At the infirmary, Miss Partridge set her down gently on one of the beds. Like all the other buildings in camp, the infirmary was another log cabin that had five beds in it. There was a tiny room at one end where the nurse slept, and another tiny room at the other end where she kept her medical supplies. There were no other occupants in any of the beds.

"Miss Frances is having her lunch now," said Miss Partridge. "She'll be back in a few minutes. You're our first casualty this summer." She stooped down and examined Laura's ankle.

"It looks like a very nasty sprain," she said. "It must have hurt you quite a bit."

"Now don't whine," Laura said to herself. "Try to be a good sport — at least!"

"Oh, it's not too bad," she said brightly.

Miss Partridge nodded. "I think I'll go and tell Miss Frances you're here," she said. "Just lie down and rest for a few minutes until she gets back." She began walking toward the door.

"Thank you," Laura said, and she summoned all her powers to smile cheerfully at Miss Partridge. She could feel that smile creaking across her face, pushing back her cheeks, and even baring her braces.

But there must have been something wrong about that smile because Miss Partridge, halfway through the door, looked at it, hesitated, and came back.

She sat down on the bed, and took Laura's hand in her own. "What's wrong, Laura?" she said, suddenly.

Laura could feel that smile dissolving quickly on her face. She just looked at Miss Partridge, not knowing what to say.

"Why didn't you tell Miss Sandra yesterday when you sprained your ankle?" continued Miss Partridge softly, and she patted Laura's hand. She wasn't smiling at all now.

And suddenly, Laura felt completely miserable. Her ankle hurt, her mosquito bites itched, her braces were tight, and she hated camp with all her heart and soul.

She told Miss Partridge everything then. She just couldn't talk fast enough. She started from the beginning, and told her about the terrible accident last December, and how Mama had been in the hospital ever since. About Aunt Minnie who came to take care of them while Mama was away, and how they had to go to camp this summer because Aunt Minnie went on a vacation. She told Miss Partridge about Anne, and how they had been separated. About her resolve to be a good sport. About Arts and Crafts, and every other thing large and small that had gone wrong. Her braces, the mosquito bites — everything. And, to tie up all the loose ends, she told Miss Partridge that she was sick of hearing about the Indians, and not at all interested in nature.

Miss Partridge held her hand all the time she was talking, nodding her head from time to time. When Laura had finished, she continued sitting there, looking at her and waiting.

"Is that all?" she said finally.

"Yes," said Laura, feeling ashamed and somehow relieved at the same time.

Miss Partridge patted her hand once more and stood up.

"I'm going to get Miss Frances now. I think we'll let you sleep here tonight."

She paused at the doorway. "I'm glad you told me everything, Laura," she said. "You'll see — it will all work out." And she was gone.

Laura couldn't really believe that it would work out but she lay back on the bed feeling very tired and comfortably empty. She knew she had been wrong to pour out all her troubles to Miss Partridge but then nothing had gone right from the time she first arrived in camp. She hadn't been herself since she left the city, and probably wouldn't be herself until she returned to it. The city was where she belonged.

After the nurse bound up her ankle and brought her lunch, Laura slept. She slept the whole afternoon, waking only to eat her supper. Then she slept again.

When she awoke, it was very dark in the cabin, and very still. But there was somebody else in the room.

"Amy?" she asked hopefully.

"No, it's me," answered Miss Partridge, approaching the bed. "I was hoping you'd be awake. If you weren't, I would have awakened you anyway."

Laura felt a blanket being wrapped around her shoulders.

"Get up now and come with me. I want you to see something."

A sudden fear spread inside Laura. "Are you sending me home?" she asked sadly.

"No, no," said Miss Partridge impatiently, helping her out of bed. "Just lean on my shoulder. Hurry now!"

She led Laura outside into the silent night.

"Where are we going?" asked Laura, completely baffled.

"Shh — look up!" said Miss Partridge.

Laura did. She looked up into a sky that had nothing to do with any other sky she had ever seen before. This sky was a huge dome with shimmering veils of light dancing up and down its sides. All around Laura it was quiet while the camp slept, but up in the sky everything was in motion.

"What is it? What is it?" Laura cried.

"It's the northern lights," said Miss Partridge. She cleared her throat as if she was going to continue, but then changed her mind and became silent.

And it really didn't matter to Laura why it happened or what it was called. Last year on the Fourth of July, Daddy had taken the whole family to Coney Island to watch the fireworks. She had loved the brilliant, flashing colors in the sky but this was something else, something better.

For a long time, Laura stood there on one leg, leaning against Miss Partridge and watching the sky dance with lights. At last Miss Partridge took her arm and began leading her back into the cabin.

"Will I see it again?" asked Laura.

"Maybe," said Miss Partridge, "maybe not. Many people live a whole lifetime without seeing it once."

She tucked Laura into her bed, and then, awkwardly, bent down and kissed her. "It's even worth a sprained ankle, isn't it?" she said.

Letters

Dear Mama,

I hope you are feeling well, and that the heat is not bothering you too much. You probably think that I've forgotten all about you since this is really the first long letter I've written to you since coming to camp. Well, that's not so at all. Now that it looks like everything will work out, I can tell you that I didn't like camp at all the first few days, and was too miserable to write. In fact, I hated it so much that I wasn't even going to tell you about it in my letters. So now you can see — since I do mention it — that things are much better now. Please don't worry about me at all.

Right now I'm still in the infirmary. Nothing much — just a sprained ankle. You know me when it comes to sprained ankles. This time it happened because I was trying to be a star volleyball player. Which just goes to show you that sports and I don't mix. The terrible thing is that people take one look at me and they think because I'm so tall that I should be an outstanding athlete. Maybe if I was scrawny and short like Amy life would be simpler.

But please don't worry about me. I'm doing my best to get used to camp, and it really is a very nice camp. The counselors go out of their way to see that we're all enjoying ourselves. They smile a lot and try to think up interesting things to do all day long. It's also a very lovely part of the country, too, if you're interested in that sort of thing. Frankly though, I don't understand why people are always sorry for children who live in the city. We have so many wonderful things that country children don't have, and if we're ever in the mood for nature, we can just hike over to one of our parks, and enjoy it there. I think the Botanical Gardens in Bronx Park has the most beautiful flowers anywhere. I haven't seen too many flowers around here — mostly Queen-Anne's-lace and some goldenrod, but Miss Partridge, the director, says there are more in the spring.

She is, incidentally, a very interesting person. You'd like her too although you might think she dresses strangely for a woman her age. She told me that she used to be a geologist and she certainly knows a lot about nature. She keeps bringing me books about flowers and trees and birds so that I'll have something to do while I'm in the infirmary. I'm really very grateful to her — she's so considerate of me. Actually, I thought I might have a chance to start reading *Matorni's Vineyard* while I was here but I don't want to hurt her feelings so I'll finish her books first. Chances are I'll be here a few days longer. I forgot to mention to you that I also caught a cold. Nothing to worry about — the fever is almost gone, and my throat is just a little sore now.

It's strange though how sometimes you can think you are as miserable as you can possibly be, and then discover how really much more miserable you can become. When I first started out on the bus to camp, I didn't think anything could be worse, but I was wrong! I'm telling you all this, Mama darling, because it all has a happy ending — otherwise I wouldn't be telling you. I met a girl on the bus named Anne Sherman who is twelve, and we liked each other right away. But once we got to camp I was put in the bunk with the eleven-year-olds, and she went with the twelves. Instead of having Anne for a bunkmate, I got Paula, Anne's kid sister, who is pretty much on Amy's order — maybe even worse. I did my best to be a good sport but things went from bad to worse.

Anyway, Miss Partridge told me today that she feels I should be transferred to the twelves. She says justice should be tempered with mercy, and that she can see I'm advanced for my age. That's the happy ending I was talking about.

Anne has been over to see me two times already. She's been telling me all about the girls in my new bunk. She said she didn't meet anybody she liked as much as me. They sound like very nice girls and I'm sure I'm going to like them all very much. My old counselor, Miss Sandra, came to visit me too. She said she was sorry I was going but she supposed it was all for the best, and that I probably should be with an older group. She seemed so friendly that I feel almost sorry she won't be my counselor anymore although I don't think we hit it off so well at the beginning.

I haven't said anything about Amy but you don't have to worry about her at all. She loves camp. She was a little homesick the first night but she's over it now. She's learning to swim and says she now knows how to float on her back. But I guess she wrote you all about that. Did she tell you about Fred, the pet snake, her bunk is taking care of?

Imagine — she doesn't mind holding it and wrapping it around her shoulders. Naturally it's only a garter snake. At least I think it's a garter snake.

Lunchtime! They've been bringing me my meals on a tray like a princess in the Arabian Nights. Smells like hot dogs — Yum! Troubles never seem to affect my appetite. I'll be writing soon. I send you a million hugs and kisses.

Your loving daughter,
Laura

P.S. I nearly forgot to tell you about the northern lights. Do you know that your daughter is one of the few lucky people in the world who has seen it? One of the books Miss Partridge gave me said it was due to sunspots but that doesn't seem like enough of a reason for such a glorious thing. I saw it the night I came here. Doesn't it sound like a fairy tale? I mean, the poor, downtrodden princess, bruised and battered from wandering in the briars — looks up at the sky, sees the northern lights, and feels hope for the first time. Not that I felt hope when I saw it. I didn't feel hope until Miss Partridge said I was going to the twelves. The only thing I felt then was that I never in all my life saw such a wonderful sky — not even in the Bronx.

P.P.S. They were hot dogs. But now they're cold dogs.

July 11

Dear Rosa,

How are you feeling? I am feeling fine. I miss you too. The girls up here are very nice but there is nothing like the old friends. I wish you were here.

I go swimming every day and yesterday we went fishing from rowboats and I caught a fish. Nobody else caught anything, and I was so excited I nearly upset the boat. The fish was too small so we had to throw it back and we had hamburgers for supper instead of fish.

I like it here very much. Laura is having the most fun of all. She has all the luck. First she sprained her ankle and caught a cold and is still sleeping in the infirmary. They bring her her meals on a tray. Then they said when she gets better she can go to the twelve bunk even though she is only eleven. Yesterday my father called the camp. He was worried because of something Laura wrote in a letter to my mother. Laura says she doesn't know why. Anyway, they came and got Laura in a hurry in the pickup truck and she got to talk to my father on the phone. Then he saw she was all right. Nobody called me though.

Anyway, I like it here very much. We are going on an overnight hike next week. Do you go swimming at the pool?
N.T.N.M.E.O.K.

Your friend,
Amy

P.S. That means 9×9 makes 81 kisses.

P.P.S. Our bunk has a pet snake named Fred. He is a rattlesnake but the ranger removed the poison so he is harmless and very affectionate. I think he likes me the best.

P.P.P.S. Did you go to the movies last Saturday? What was playing?

July 11

Dear Daddy,

I hope you are well and not worried anymore. You sounded so upset over the phone but I still can't figure out what I said in my letter to Mama to give you both the idea that anything was wrong. How is Mama? When will she be able to get out of bed?

My ankle is all better now, and my cold is just about gone. Tomorrow the nurse says they are going to throw me out of here. She says she is tired of looking at my face all the time. Of course, she's being funny.

Mama told you that I was going to be transferred to the twelve bunk, didn't she? Did she tell you about my new friend, Anne Sherman? I wish I had a camera so I could send you a picture of the two of us together. We are exactly the same height — our hair and eyes are the same color, and I think we could pass for sisters. Anne is thinner than I am, though, and her teeth are beautiful. As a matter of fact, she's a very pretty girl but we do look alike anyway. She says I look like Joan

73

Crawford, the actress, and if I had a permanent, I'd look even more like her. Now that I think of it, Mama looks something like Joan Crawford, doesn't she? And I'm supposed to look like Mama.

Sometimes I wonder though. Mama keeps saying she looked exactly like me when she was my age but from that picture she has of herself when she was eleven — you know, the one with Grandma — I can't see it. She's so slim and pretty in the picture, and her teeth were always straight. Do you think she only says it to make me feel good? You can tell me the truth, Daddy. I won't feel bad, and I won't tell Mama. She doesn't like me to think I'm not pretty, and there's no point in making her feel bad.

I think girls worry too much about their looks, anyway. Brains are more important than beauty. If I could only have straight teeth, it wouldn't bother me at all what the rest of my face looked like. Right now the braces are still very annoying but not as much as before. Sometimes I think everybody is looking at them, and then I feel like I'm just all braces with legs and arms. But other times I practically forget I'm wearing them. I keep telling myself that once my teeth are straight nobody will ever say "Buck teeth" to me again. Won't that be something!

But getting back to Anne — I like her very much, and am so happy she's my friend. She's been visiting me at the infirmary as much as she can, and we talk and talk and talk and talk. What's so funny is that I never thought I would like a girl like Anne. Not only because she's so pretty but also because she's different from my friends in the city like Sally Robinson or Marjorie Kahn. She's not good in school. She doesn't even like school. She's going to take a commercial course in high school and then plans to be a secretary and marry a rich man. She doesn't read many books either except for mysteries. When we talk about how much I read or how good I am in school, I feel almost stupid being so smart. But she says it's very nice being so good in school although she doesn't understand how anybody could enjoy history or English. She said she always thought the girls who were good in school were snobs and kind of boring to be with. But she doesn't think I'm that way at all.

She likes sports and is very much interested in the movies. Her hobby is collecting pictures of movie stars and pasting them into an album. She even brought the album to camp because she didn't feel it would be safe at home. We've been looking through the album together and I don't mind very much. She's so much fun to be with that it doesn't seem to matter what we're doing.

Anne says the other girls in the bunk are also interested in sports and play a lot of punchball. She says they're all pleased I'm coming since with me there will be ten girls, which means they can have two even teams. I told Anne immediately that I am absolutely no good at all in any kind of sports. I decided I'd better make that clear right at the start. But she just kept on saying she knew I'd like it once I learned how, and that she thought I had a good build for punchball. So here we go again!

Today I sat outside in the sunshine and tried to see if I could tell one tree from the other. There are birches here, oaks, maples, pine, and I could spot them without any trouble at all. At first when Miss Partridge brought me all those nature books I felt kind of disappointed because I've been dying to read *Matorni's Vineyard* — and still am. But it's like a game, being able to tell one tree from another. Before, they all looked the same to me. Right now, I'm working on the birds. I saw an indigo bunting go by before, and Miss Partridge says it's kind of rare around here. She says they'll make a real nature lover out of me before the end of the summer. I don't know about that but I do enjoy reading about nature in books. Anyway, after I come home from camp, I'll take you on a tour of Crotona Park and tell you the names of the different trees and birds. I can hardly wait for September.

All my love and lots of x x x x x x xs,

Laura

P.S. I'd like to make something for Mama in the Arts and Crafts shop before I come home. Do you think she would like a handwoven belt? I'm thinking of making a necklace for Aunt Minnie based on an Indian necklace made of wolves' teeth. Miss Rosalie, the Arts and Crafts counselor, wears one. She used chicken bones instead of wolves' teeth and nobody would ever guess it was chicken bones.

P.P.S. How do you like your own cooking?

P.P.P.S. S.W.A.K.

The Lair of the Bear

There were two signs over the bunkhouse that stated "LAIR OF THE BEAR" and "BEWARE!"

"The girls got that up yesterday," said Miss Susan, who was escorting Laura over from the infirmary to her new bunk.

Laura grinned. She knew that every bunk at camp took the name of an animal native to North America, and familiar to the Indians. The elevens had been the wolves. "Better to be a bear than wolf," she thought.

"They're resting now," Miss Susan said softly as she opened the door of the cabin, and led the way inside.

Something dropped down from above, and splattered them with water. Miss Susan, particularly, must have been a perfect target for the can of water when it dropped because she stood there, her hair drenched, coughing and spluttering, while the water ran down her face.

"Betty!" she finally yelled.

"Who, me?" came an innocent voice from one end of the room.

"So that's Betty," Laura thought good-naturedly, brushing the water from her shoulders.

"Do you realize," Miss Susan continued angrily, "that Laura has just recovered from a bad cold? This is not funny. It's never funny, and unless you stop these stupid jokes yourself, we'll have to find some way of making you stop."

"Who, me?" said Betty.

"Now you can just go get the mop, and clean all this mess up," scolded Miss Susan. "And this afternoon, you'll skip swimming, and spend your time at KP."

"Everybody blames me," said Betty pitifully. But she got up from her bed, slipped into her sandals, and went off to find the mop.

"We didn't even see her do it this time," Anne said, smiling and waving at Laura from across the room. "That Betty!"

"And don't think," Miss Susan continued, "that I don't know who put sheets over their heads last night and went and scared the eight-year-olds while I was in the Rec Hall."

There was absolute silence in the bunk, but Laura could see a few of the girls looking at each other out of the corners of their eyes. She hadn't heard about this particular prank from Anne but she had heard enough about Betty and her practical jokes to fit all the evidence together.

"Very funny — going and scaring little kids and making them cry! Just because she thinks up these silly jokes doesn't mean you all have to go along with her."

"We really didn't see her set up the can of water this time," said a big, pleasant-looking girl who Laura realized must be Florence. "Honestly, Miss Susan, we didn't."

"Well . . ." Miss Susan brushed off enough water from one arm to put it around Laura's shoulder. "Anyway, here's Laura. She probably thinks she stumbled into an insane asylum."

"Hi, everybody," Laura said shyly, looking around at her new bunkmates. From Anne's description, Laura could pick out many of them before Miss Susan even said their names. Florence, the biggest girl — everybody liked her. The redheaded Helen — "drippy," Anne said, but not too bad. Rachel with the blond curls — "very sensitive." Lilly — freckles and "lots of fun." Joan — fat but a fast runner. . . .

"You can have the bed next to Anne's," Miss Susan said, beginning to smile again. "Lilly used to sleep there but she doesn't mind changing."

"Thanks, Lilly," Laura said gratefully.

"Oh, it's all right." Lilly shrugged. "I wanted to sleep near Rachel and besides Anne snores."

"I'm going to change now," Miss Susan said, walking off to the little cubicle where she slept. "You'd better get into some other clothes too."

Laura's suitcase stood near her bed, and she opened it and pulled out some dry clothes. The other girls watched as she began undressing. This was one aspect of camp life she didn't think she'd ever get used to — this dressing and undressing in front of a bunch of people. Some girls didn't seem to mind but she did. Especially now that all these changes in her body were taking place. If she faced the wall while she dressed, everybody could see her back but if her back was to the wall they could see her front. Laura faced the wall, and quickly changed into a dry pair of shorts and shirt.

"I'll bet you're nearly as tall as I am," Florence said, appraisingly. She and Laura stood back to back while Anne measured them. Florence was a few inches taller.

"She's just my size," said Anne, "and she's not even twelve."

A few uncomfortable moments passed for Laura while the group continued its inspection.

"Why don't you get your things unpacked?" Mary said hungrily.

Laura nodded and thought to herself, "Mary, Mary . . . what did Anne say about Mary?" She opened her suitcase, and pulled out her books, which lay on top of her clothes. The girls watched as she put them on top of the orange crate next to her bed.

"Books!" said Mary.

"Laura reads a lot," Anne said quickly, "but she's lots of fun."

"What's that red one?" Mary asked, getting off her bed, and holding out her hand.

"It's called *Matorni's Vineyard*," Laura explained, handing the book over to Mary. She watched Mary fingering the handsome red cover and the gilt print. Then she remembered what Anne had said about Mary. Mary liked to trade — everything — clothes, pencils, paper, candy, anything. Probably books too.

"It's my mother's book," Laura said firmly. "It belongs to a set she bought before she was married. It's not mine," she added emphatically.

Mary handed the book back but came and stood near Laura, watching as the contents of the suitcase emerged.

Laura hung up her jacket on the hook next to her bed, pulled out her comb and toothbrush, and arranged some of her clothes on the bed. Mary's eyes skimmed the worn shorts and shirts, flew over the old sweater, and came to rest on Laura's blue bathing cap.

"That's a pretty color," she said.

"It's OK," Laura said, nonchalantly.

"I have a red one," continued Mary.

"Uh, huh," Laura began sliding the suitcase under her bed.

"Do you like red?" Mary said hopefully.

"Not particularly." Laura hung her bathrobe up on another hook.

"It has a white band all around it," continued Mary. "What color is your bathing suit?"

"Green."

"Mine's blue."

Laura hesitated and looked at Mary's eager face. She really preferred blue to red but she didn't think it was worth any further discussion.

"Let's see it," she said pleasantly.

In a few minutes, the transaction was completed, and Laura was the owner of a red bathing cap with a white band around it.

"You got off easy," Anne said, leaving her own bed, and flopping down on Laura's. "She got my favorite pair of shorts — orange too."

"It had a hole in it," Mary said, pushing her hair into her new blue cap, and joining Anne on the bed.

By the time Laura had all her belongings

arranged in the orange crate, Janet, Lilly, and Florence were also draped over Laura's bed. There wasn't any room left so Laura stood regarding her guests with satisfaction. What a nice, friendly bunch of girls, she thought.

Through the door came Betty, carrying a mop. "Did you tell her?" she asked, jerking her head in Laura's direction.

"Tell her what?" said Anne.

"About the initiation."

"That's right." Florence grinned. "We forgot all about it."

"Tonight," whispered Betty mysteriously, "when the moon is full."

Anne explained on the way down to the lake. "It was Betty's idea. All of us went through it. Before you can be a full-fledged member of the Lair of the Bear you have to go through an initiation ceremony."

"What do I have to do?" asked Laura nervously.

"Oh — it's nothing," Anne laughed. "After we're all supposed to be in bed, and Miss Susan goes off to the Rec Hall, they blindfold you and take you outside. Everybody makes all sorts of crazy noises and tries to scare you. The thing is to stay absolutely quiet." She lowered her voice. "Then they hand you the end of a ball of string and tell you to follow it. Somebody's holding the ball but you're not supposed to know it, and they lead you all over the place. Don't worry — there's nothing to it."

Miss Susan decided that Laura had better take it easy for one more day. So, while her bunkmates were swimming, she found a dry, comfortable spot near the lake and glanced through the last book Miss Partridge had given her on wild flowers. Every so often, Anne came out of the water, and stood over her, dribbling water down on her neck in a friendly way. Later, with Laura watching from another dry, comfortable spot, the girls played punchball.

"There's really nothing very complicated about the game," Laura thought, observing the logical sequence of punching the ball, running around the bases, and arriving at home plate without being tagged. It looked easy too. She watched Rachel throw the ball up in the air, whack it, and dash off to first base. Out in the field, Anne scooped up the ball, tossed it to Mary, the first baseman, who tagged Rachel just as she landed on base.

"Out!" yelled Mary.

"Safe!" screamed Rachel.

"Out!" judged Miss Susan.

"Time!" roared Rachel's teammates as they left home plate to come and argue with Miss Susan over her decision. Their indignant voices rose higher and higher. Mary's teammates left their positions in the field, and joined the shouting, hand-waving group.

"Imagine getting so worked up over a game," Laura thought, but as she watched them, she suddenly felt a great longing to be part of that group, and to really care about whether or not a player was "safe" or "out."

Miss Susan's decision remained firm, and the game resumed after some intense grumbling on the part of Rachel and her teammates.

"Tomorrow," Laura thought, "I'm really going to try. Nothing is impossible if you put your mind to it." And as she watched the game unfold, she could imagine herself right along in there with the rest of them, punching, running, and shouting — just like anyone else.

That night, everybody was in bed before taps sounded. Not a complaint or a giggle issued from any of the motionless figures. Miss Susan stood in the middle of the cabin, and moved her flashlight around, illuminating each bed. The silence was unnatural, and to her trained ear, suspicious.

"Now listen!" she said. "Don't try anything funny tonight."

She turned the light of her flashlight on the bed where Betty slept. "There's a limit to my good nature." At suppertime, somebody had put sugar into the salt shakers, and salt into the sugar bowl. Since Betty had been engaged upon KP the entire afternoon, the finger of suspicion naturally pointed in her direction. But now, Betty's face lay composed in sleep, her eyes shut, her mouth open, breathing deep, regular breaths.

Miss Susan stood a few moments longer and then walked slowly to the door. She paused and said, "Any more high jinks tonight and there won't be any swimming for a whole week. Good night, all."

"Good night, Miss Susan," came a chorus of very sleepy voices.

Miss Susan's footsteps could be heard crunching away into the distance. Nobody stirred. Finally a whisper from Mary. "Well?"

"Shh!" from Betty. "She'll be back. Stay down!"

Sure enough, from the silence outside, a slow, furtive, crunching that came closer and closer. The door edged open little by little, and there stood Miss Susan, her flashlight again making the rounds. A few of the girls tossed in deep sleep as the light played upon their beds. Finally darkness settled down upon them again, and the crunching footsteps, faster and firmer this time, finally merged with the other night sounds.

"Stay still a while," Betty ordered. "Just in case."

Laura lay rigid in her bed, feeling a delicious sense of importance. Just think — all the evening's activities centered around her. All the mysterious preparations and giggles that had grown in intensity since suppertime were in her behalf.

Of course, it was all so ridiculous and yet she couldn't help feeling excited and pleased. The only club she had ever belonged to before was the History Club in school, and never in her whole life had she been involved in an initiation. These girls certainly were a lively bunch, but she liked them. Naturally, Anne the most, but all the rest too. Well — maybe not Betty so much but then it just might have been her imagination. Before bedtime that night, while she was brushing her teeth, she noticed Betty acting peculiarly. Betty was making strangling noises while brushing her own teeth. She was also holding her toothbrush with both hands and sawing away at her upper teeth which she had stuck all the way out. Probably doesn't mean a thing, Laura thought quickly, and turned her thoughts to more pleasant matters. After the initiation, she would be a real member of the group. Maybe tomorrow she could try parting her hair on the side, the way Anne did. Really, the shape of her face was very much like Anne's so maybe wearing her hair a different way would make a dramatic improvement in her appearance. Then her socks. She'd never particularly noticed before that most girls her age wore the cuffs up and not down the way she did. Probably make her legs look thinner if she did. Then the other girls wore their shirts out, not tucked in, the way she did. How was it that she had never noticed these things before?

A rustling from Betty's end of the room, and Laura licked her braces expectantly. A flashlight glimmered, and Betty's voice ordered, "Now be careful, and quiet. She's suspicious, and if she catches us, our goose is cooked.

"Very well." Betty's voice assumed a deep, somber tone. "Will the sisters bring forward the candidate."

Three or four pairs of hands yanked off the bedclothes, and pulled Laura to her feet.

"Put on your slippers and your jacket," Anne whispered, and patted Laura's arm.

Laura obeyed, thinking fond, happy thoughts about Anne. Then she was dragged forward to Betty who now sat, cross-legged, wrapped in a blanket on top of an orange crate.

"Blindfold her!" ordered Betty.

Laura smiled as a scarf was wrapped securely around her eyes. It was all so silly and so nice.

"Candidate!" Betty's voice growled. "You desire to be a member of the Lair of the Bear? Is it not so? Speak!"

"Yes," laughed Laura.

"Do not laugh!" hissed Betty. "You are

in the jaws of death, and if you laugh, it will be your last laugh."

Laura composed that part of her face which showed, while a few giggles came from behind her.

"Silence!" rumbled Betty. "Those who would belong to the sacred, saintly, solemn, secret sisterhood of the Lair of the Bear must be willing to undergo tortures unknown to most humans. They must endure suffering, and fight evil spirits, and obey everything that is asked of them. They must neither laugh nor speak during their trial. Do you agree?"

"Yes," Laura whispered, trying her best not to smile.

"Think before you decide. For once you say yes, you may not change your mind. And if you fail . . ." A wicked, witchlike laugh nearly forced Laura to burst out laughing but she clenched her teeth, and held her breath. "Well, Candidate, do you agree?"

"Yes!"

"Remember." Betty's voice dropped to an eerie whisper. "You must not speak or you die. No matter what is said to you. No matter who questions you. No matter what mon-

ster torments you . . . you must not speak!
Do you understand?"

Laura nodded.

"Then let the rites begin," chanted Betty.

A low moaning, broken occasionally by
giggles, filled the room as Betty said, "Those
cries are from the candidates who failed.
They are doomed to spend eternity in the
snake pit right at your feet. One false step
and you fall to your doom. At this very moment, one of the snakes has crawled out of
the pit and is at your foot. Do not move!"
Something wet wrapped itself around
Laura's ankle, and, without thinking, she
jerked her foot away. Immediately, she felt
a jab, like a pin prick on her ankle.

"Tsk, tsk," came Betty's voice from below. "You were warned, and you failed to
take heed. Already the poison from the
snake's fangs is spreading, spreading
through your body. In two minutes, you will
be dead unless . . ." The wet thing was removed from her foot. "Unless you eat the
snake that stung you. Do you wish to live?"

Laura nodded, and thought pleasantly,
"My, she's good at this."

"Well then, reach out your hand, and eat
the slimy, slithering serpent. Eat!"

Laura stretched out her hand, and felt a mass of cold, clammy goo. "Ugh!" she thought, shuddering, and pulling her hand back.

"Eat!" ordered the voice.

Cautiously, Laura reached out and gingerly picked up some of the gooey stuff. The stifled giggles around her were reassuring. Most of it fell out of her hand but she raised what remained to her mouth, and slowly licked it. Jell-O. Thank goodness.

Suddenly, Laura heard a good deal of scuffling, and strained her ears to understand what was happening next.

"Next, O Candidate, you must show if you have courage. We ask you to leap head-first into the pit of knives. Only those who are worthy to belong to the Lair of the Bear can attempt this feat, and emerge unharmed. But those who have evil ways . . ." Here Betty laughed her wicked, witchlike laugh again.

Some of the girls prodded Laura up on top of what was obviously one of the beds.

"Now leap!" Betty commanded. "But remember — headfirst."

Laura stood at the brink of the bed, and reflected nervously that this really wasn't a very good idea. She might break her neck. She might even crack her braces.

"Jump!" snapped Betty in a fierce voice.

"Darn her!" thought Laura, but she dove down, head first, her arms around her head, and her lips sucked in protectively around her braces. Buff. Into what must have been stacks of pillows, Laura's flight ended.

"What a baby I am," she thought happily, scrambling to her feet. "Anne said there was nothing to worry about." She straightened herself up, and determined to do just as she was told without question.

"Next, the cavern of the vampire bats," came Betty's deep, sepulchral voice.

Hands turned Laura in another direction, and began prodding.

"Walk — but beware!"

Laura started walking, and suddenly felt something soft and furry lapping at her face.

"Uuuh," she thought squeamishly, "it really feels like bats. Wonder what it is." But she continued walking.

"Watch out," suddenly hissed Betty, "you're walking into a stalactite."

Laura stopped but too late. Something

bopped her on the head, and her cheek became wet and sticky.

"Blood," drawled Betty.

Laura put up her hand, and wiped her face. A familiar smell dribbled down under her nose. Ketchup. Well, she'd certainly have to wash her hair tomorrow. Somebody was giggling right next to her. She wiped her face, feeling the ketchup spreading all over her. More giggles. "I must be a mess," she thought tolerantly.

"And now," Betty droned, "the final and most dangerous test. Take her outside," she ordered, and, lowering her voice, said to her confederates, "and for Pete's sake be quiet. If we're caught, we'll really get it this time."

Out into the cool night air, Laura was propelled. A string was placed in her hand.

"All alone," whispered Betty, "you must follow this ball of string through the cave of the twelve-headed monster. All alone you must go until you reach the end of the string. There you must wait — if you are still alive — silent and motionless, regardless of what evil spirits speak to you. Then if the sisterhood agree you have passed the tests they will come and lead you back in triumph."

"Watch out, Laura!" A low cry issued from one side of her. "There's a wolf behind you."

"Sure, sure," Laura thought pleasantly.

"I throw the ball into the cave," Betty spoke solemnly. "Go now, alone, and follow where it leads."

Laura, holding the string, started off and walked smack into a tree. Loud laughter behind her.

"Shh, shh!" somebody whispered.

She rubbed her nose, and wondered how much longer it was going to go on. Walking more slowly now, Laura felt tall grass around her ankles.

"I must be right behind the bunkhouse," she thought.

"Hey!" She heard Anne's voice. "Someone's coming. Everybody duck in the bushes. Here, Laura, take off the blindfold. Come here!"

"Sure, sure," thought Laura. She heard scrambling all around her on her right but the string seemed to be tugging on the left. Obediently, she followed it, stepped off into nowhere, and went rolling down a hill. She held on to the string though, and when she finally reached the bottom, was gratified to find it still clutched tightly in her hand. Slightly bruised, and considerably shaken, she scrambled to her feet, thinking that this was getting rough now.

"Don't grumble," she scolded to herself. "The others have gone through this too."

Her pajama bottoms were torn at the knees, and she could feel raw scratches on both kneecaps. Blood too — not ketchup. "Oh well, it will soon be over," she supposed. She started following the string again, walking very slowly. The trail still led downward but the slope seemed less steep than the one she had tumbled over. The string was tugging now, and she followed it into some high bushes where suddenly it ended. With surprise, she felt the end of it but there was nobody holding it as Anne had said. Laura became thoughtful and a little hurt too. Why had Anne fibbed that way? Her foot rested on a rock, and she knelt down, and felt a large, flat stone on the ground. "Oh," she thought, understanding everything now. This must be a sacrificial altar, or something like it where the initiation would be completed. "Anne probably wanted me to be surprised." She sat down on the stone and waited. She could hear none of the familiar giggles that had attended her up until now, but she did hear quite a bit of thrashing around in the bushes around her.

"They're probably up to something real fiendish," she thought with amusement. "What a bunch! They certainly make it exciting."

A low voice that seemed to come from high above her called, "Laura, Laura, where are you?"

"They know very well where I am," Laura thought, and she remained silent and motionless as ordered.

Next, she heard some scrambling, tumbling noises, a little closer.

"Here they come," she thought.

"Laura, Laura," a few voices called, louder this time. "Oh, what happened to her? Where is she?" This was Anne's voice.

"They're really doing everything to get me to talk." Laura could hear them quite clearly. "They must be standing right on the other side of the bushes."

"I'll just die if anything happened to her." Anne's voice again, high and whining.

"She's good," Laura thought approvingly, and waited for them to come and get her.

Florence spoke now. "Come on, we'll have to get help. Hurry!" The noises receded.

Laura felt disappointed. She was tired of sitting on the cold stone, and growing just slightly bored with the whole business. Really — hadn't it gone on long enough? Not that she was complaining, though. She hoped that she would come through the initiation as successfully as anyone else, and she certainly didn't want anyone to think she was a bad sport. But to herself she could say that, with a little more imagination, the initiation might have been more interesting. Too much falling, and crashing, and loud noises. Sort of like one of those silly Laurel and Hardy movies. Not that she would ever say anything to the girls — well — maybe just to Anne. . . .

A sudden movement from the other side of the rock startled her, and she turned her blindfolded face in the direction of the sound.

"Now what are they up to?"

But nothing happened. A stillness which seemed to contain someone else beside herself and then a scurrying sound in the bushes. "Trying to make me think that's a wild animal," Laura thought, yawning, suddenly very sleepy. She snuggled down inside her warm jacket, and must have dozed off because the next thing she heard was loud voices all around her. "Laura! Laura! Laura!"

It even sounded as if Miss Susan and some other adults were shouting along with her bunkmates. Now, wasn't that odd! Was the whole camp in on the initiation? Laura couldn't help feeling a strong sense of disapproval. It just didn't seem proper for grownups to take part in this kind of kid stuff. However, she remained silent. Even when she heard somebody shout, "Look, here's the string," and felt the bushes give way, and lots of hands all over her, she did not smile, and she did not speak.

"Oh, Laura, Laura," Anne was sobbing, and pulled off the blindfold.

By the light of many flashlights, Laura could see all the girls looking down at her. And there was Miss Susan, and my goodness, Miss Partridge too, and quite a few others. Laura blinked, and began wondering if something had gone wrong.

Miss Partridge quickly knelt by her side,

and cradled Laura's head on her bony shoulder. "Thank goodness, you're safe. Thank goodness." Her hands gently began to poke and prod all over Laura's body. "Where does it hurt?" she asked tenderly.

"Blood! There's blood on her face," cried Miss Susan.

"Oh, Laura, say something," Anne sobbed.

"State of shock," somebody whispered.

Very confused, Laura looked up into the half-lighted faces above her.

"Is it over?" she asked uncertainly.

Conversations

"Mrs. Roosevelt," said Anne. "I'm sure Mrs. Roosevelt never was much good at sports."

Laura finished sprinkling the disinfectant down the first privy, and went on to the next.

"And Florence Nightingale," continued Anne, pausing in her work, and resting the long brush on the floor. "I never heard anybody mention that Florence Nightingale was an athlete."

Laura banged the door of the second privy behind her and began sprinkling again.

"And what about Martha Washington?" inquired Anne, waiting in vain for an answer, and hearing only the shlop, shlop of Laura's scrubbing brush.

"And that one who wrote about the moors — you know — Laurence Olivier was in the movie. Heathcliff! Heathcliff!" Anne intoned.

"Emily Brontë," Laura said savagely, *"Wuthering Heights."*

"See that," Anne said encouragingly. "Just name a book, and you know right off who wrote it. Aw, Laura!"

Laura emerged from the second privy, and looked straight in Anne's face.

"Don't try to cheer me up," she snapped. "The only thing I'm good for is . . . is . . . this." Laura waved the arm with the brush in a descriptive arc around the latrine.

"Well," said Anne sensibly, "we've been doing it for nearly a whole week. We ought to be good at it."

"Nobody," continued Laura in a desperate voice, "likes me anymore. You're the only one who tries to be nice, and you're only doing it out of pity."

"Well," said Anne cautiously, "the girls are a little annoyed at you but it'll blow over. I remember when Betty put toothpaste in everybody's slippers. Nobody talked to her for a few days. They'll forget all about it in a couple of days. You'll see."

"No, they won't," Laura cried, leaning against the privy door, and shutting her eyes. "For a whole week we're assigned to KP and this. And then for a whole week we can't go swimming and we all have to be in bed at seven o'clock. And it's all my fault."

"They'll forget about it, you'll see," Anne repeated soothingly.

"Why, why?" Laura moaned. "Why didn't I answer? How could I be so stupid? Why do I always have to be different from everybody else?"

"You were only doing," recited Anne patiently, as if she knew this particular speech by heart, "what the girls told you to do. They said not to say anything whatever happened, and that," Anne sighed, "is just what you did. How would you know that Betty dropped the ball of string?" Her voice became thoughtful. "What I don't understand is that night while we were looking for you, when everybody thought you must have been dead, Miss Susan sounded as if she thought you were the greatest person in the whole world, and Miss Partridge said something like if they only found you in one piece, she wouldn't care about anything else. But when they did find you, and everything was fine, they were so mad, they couldn't hand out punishments fast enough."

"Maybe," Laura said darkly, "it would have been better if something did happen to me."

"No," Anne said reasonably, "it probably would have been worse. They would have had to close the camp, and maybe all the girls would have to go to jail for murder. No!" Anne shook her head firmly. "It's better this way. Besides," she smiled lovingly at Laura, "what would I do without you?"

"Oh, you'd manage," Laura grumbled. "Everybody likes you. What do you need me for?"

"Aw, Laura."

"Sure, I know you're sorry for me so you always take my part. But that's all right." Laura straightened herself up, and shrugged her shoulders. "I can get along by myself. I know you're dying to be with the others, laughing at their jokes, having a good time. Go ahead!" Laura waved her brush toward the door. "Don't worry about me. I don't need your pity."

Anne sighed. "Gee, you sound like Ida Lupino in that movie with John Garfield where she's a gun moll, and he's in love with her, and she tells him. . . ."

"All the girls," Laura interrupted fiercely, "want to be your friend. Even Florence always tries to sit near you in the mess hall. And Lilly . . . Well, I know how much fun you and Lilly used to have when she slept next to you. You said so yourself. You two were always laughing and telling jokes long after everybody else fell asleep."

"Yes, we sure did," Anne agreed, "but Laura, I like you better than Lilly."

"Why?" Laura cried. "Why?"

Anne shrugged her shoulders. "Because I do."

Betty came through the door. "Hi, Anne," she said. "Hi, Babe Ruth."

"My name," said Laura carefully, "is not Babe Ruth."

"Oh," Betty said innocently, "did I say Babe Ruth?"

"Yes," Laura said between her teeth, "you said Babe Ruth."

Betty picked up the trash can, and began moving off with it. "I'm getting charley horsed from carrying all these cans," she

said. "G'bye, Anne. G'bye, Babe . . . oops . . .
I mean, Laura."

Laura looked after the departing figure
with hate. If she could only think of something withering to say to Betty. But the
trouble was, she never could, or if she did,
it was always too late. Take the way Betty
always used to stick her teeth out while they
brushed their teeth. For a couple of days,
all Laura could think of was to act indifferent but finally she'd thought up a perfect
remark to make next time it happened. She
would look Betty straight in the eye, smile
sweetly, and say in a loud, casual voice for
everybody to hear, "I didn't know you had
so many teeth, Betty. The way you act, I
thought you only had a couple of baby
teeth." That would stop her in her tracks,
and all the girls would laugh at her for a
change. But wouldn't you know. Now that
Laura was actually waiting for Betty to
stick out her teeth, just one more time, Betty
stopped doing it altogether. Now she just
kept calling Laura "Babe Ruth," and Laura
hadn't been able to think up a single smart
answer.

"I hate her," Laura said out loud.

"She sure can be a pain in the neck,"

Anne agreed. "But don't mind it if she calls you Babe Ruth." She giggled but quickly stopped when she saw Laura's unhappy face. "That's what I was trying to tell you before. All those famous women — none of them probably were good at sports either."

Laura picked up her brush, and disappeared into the third privy, closing the door behind her.

"The important thing," Anne continued, looking earnestly at the door, "is that you try. That's what Miss Susan said — if a person tries her best, that's the most anybody can ask of her."

The sounds of furious scrubbing started up again.

"After all," Anne went on, "if a person is very smart, that's more important than being able to play punchball. Besides, you've only been playing for a week, and maybe you need a little more time." She opened the door, and watched Laura's back moving vigorously in time with the scrubbing brush.

"You did," she said encouragingly, "get on base once yesterday."

Laura just turned and regarded her with a disgusted look.

"Well, yes, I know." A pained note entered

Anne's voice. "And why you turned around when you were nearly home, and went back to third base, when Florence was right behind you, and I was right behind Florence ..."

Laura groaned. "I forgot to touch third," she said in a weak voice.

"We nearly scored three runs," Anne continued, the anguish now plain in her voice. "We would have won. The last inning. ..." Her voice drifted off.

Laura put the scrubbing brush down, and took Anne's hand. "Maybe," she said hopefully, "I won't be on your team today."

Anne managed a smile but her hand hung limp in Laura's.

"After all," Laura continued with energy, "it's not fair that I should always be on your team. Yesterday I messed up your home run, and the day before I ran into you just when you caught that fly ball, and the day before I ..."

"Never mind *that*," Anne murmured.

"No," Laura went on hotly. "What's fair is fair. After all, you're a person too. You've got feelings. Why should you always be on the same team with me? No, I've decided," she said, waving off a feeble attempt on

Anne's part to interrupt. "I'm going to talk to Miss Susan and insist that she put me on another team. So you just cheer up." Laura smiled, and squeezed Anne's hand. "Let me take care of it."

"Thanks, Laura," Anne said, returning the squeeze. "But forget it. She won't."

"Won't what?"

"Won't put you on another team."

"Why not?"

"Because she decided a few days ago that until you kind of — you know — get the feel of the game, you'd better play on the same team with Florence and me."

"Oh!"

"Florence is twice as good as anyone else, Miss Susan said, so it sort of balances out."

"But we keep losing."

"That's right, and I can't figure why. If Florence is twice as good as anyone else and you — well — you still don't have the feel of the game — wouldn't that mean that 50 percent of the time we should win anyway?"

"No," Laura said gloomily. "Florence is only twice as good as anybody else, and I'm ten times worse."

Anne picked up her brush and retired into the third privy.

"Aw, Anne." Laura thought deeply for a few moments. "You know," she said, "I've got an idea."

The rhythmic shlop, shlop of the scrubbing brush continued.

"Why couldn't I be umpire?"

Anne opened the door and looked at Laura with interest.

"That way," Laura continued, "I'd still be in the game but we'd all be a lot happier. Miss Susan probably wouldn't mind taking a rest from being umpire, and the teams could be the way they were before I came. Florence's team would have four girls, and Lilly's five."

Anne nodded vigorously. "That's a great idea," she said. "Great!"

They beamed at each other.

"Let's go ask her right now. I bet she'll say yes."

"Maybe we ought to finish up first," Anne said. "She'll be in a better mood if we do."

Rachel came through the door, carrying a load of paper supplies. "Whew, is it hot!" she complained. "And we can't go swimming for another three days." She looked pointedly at Laura.

"Say, Rachel," Anne said happily, "Laura wants to be umpire."

"What?"

"She'd rather be umpire than play."

Rachel put down the paper supplies. She smiled at Laura. "That's great," she said, and hurried to the door. "Florence! Oh, Florence!" she shouted.

"What?" came a distant voice.

"Laura wants to be umpire."

"What!"

"Come here."

Florence hurried through the door. "What did you say?"

"Laura wants to be umpire."

"Ah!"

Rachel and Florence looked at Laura as if they were seeing her for the first time, and also, as if they liked what they saw.

"Does Helen know?"

"I didn't tell anybody else yet," Laura said modestly.

"Come on, Rachel, let's go tell her." The two girls, with an approving smile at Laura, hurried off.

"See," said Anne, "I told you they wouldn't be mad at you for long."

"You know," said Laura, "I think I might even get to enjoy punchball if I don't have to play."

"Oh, you definitely will," Anne said with certainty. "You'll be a great umpire. It's like being a judge, and you're that type, anyway." She slipped her arm through Laura's and hugged. "But don't do it unless you really want to."

"I really want to," said Laura.

There was a crash and a clatter as the empty trash can came rolling in at the door. Behind it, stepping gingerly, came Betty.

"Hey, Betty," said Anne, "Laura wants ..."

"It's all over the place," Betty said sulkily.

"What's all over the place?"

"Poison ivy."

Laura and Anne exchanged significant looks. "Not again!" said Anne.

"Yes, it is." Betty was absolutely serious. "All over the path, and right here outside the door. I just stepped on it." She walked to the door, and pointed furiously outside.

Laura followed her, and looked at the innocent clump of leaves that were being accused. "That's not poison ivy," she stated.

"Yes, it is," Betty insisted.

Anne came, and peered out the door. "Even I know that's not poison ivy," she said. "You just imagine you see it. You're always wrong, anyway."

"No, I'm not."

"And besides, Laura says it's not poison ivy."

"So what? Who is she, anyway?"

"She knows all about plants. Even Miss Susan said so yesterday when we hiked to Lake Sebago. She said Laura knows more about the plants and flowers than she does. So if Laura says it's not poison ivy, then it's not poison ivy."

"You see," explained Laura kindly, Anne's praise glowing in her ears, "poison ivy has a three-leaf formation. This plant over here has only two."

"Who cares?" Betty grumbled.

"Anyway," said Anne quickly, "Laura wants to be umpire."

Betty shrugged her shoulders. "So what!"

"Well, don't you think that's a great idea?"

"No," said Betty, beginning to lose her

sulky look. "It's a terrible idea. I always made sure never to play on her team so I'll miss her."

"Oh, go fly a kite," Anne said pleasantly.

Rachel hurried in. "Are you finished yet?" she asked.

"No."

"Well, hurry up!" Rachel handed Laura her brush. "We've been reprieved. Miss Susan said she'll let us go swimming today because it's so hot. Come on, Betty, move!"

Laura held her brush, and looked at Betty in anticipation. Just this very moment as Rachel walked through the door, it came to her. What she would say when Betty said, "Bye, Babe Ruth." She would look her right in the eye, and say, "Foul!" And hold her nose.

Betty put the trash can where it belonged, and walked slowly to the door.

"Come on, Laura, hurry!" Anne urged, disappearing into the last privy.

"I'm coming, I'm coming," Laura mumbled, keeping her eyes on Betty. Oh, she could hardly wait!

Betty turned at the door, and smiled at Laura. "Bye, Anne," she said. "Bye . . . Einstein."

Rain

A damp wind blew across Laura's face, and she snuggled down deeper into her covers. Cold outside and warm inside — mmm — she was so comfortable. Reveille had sounded just a few minutes before but Laura chose to ignore it. Somebody sang:

"Rain, rain, go away
  Come again another day."

Slowly, Laura managed to open one eye. A few eager beavers had already thrown off their covers and were beginning to dress. Across from her, Anne was smiling.

118

"It's raining," she said. "The first time so far."

"That's nice," said Laura.

Slowly, she sat up in bed, listening to the hissing sound of the rain. "I could use a day off," she thought gratefully. "I'm so hoarse." Ever since she'd become umpire, over a week ago, her voice had gradually grown huskier and huskier. It really was amazing how some people would argue even when they knew they were wrong. Mary sometimes, and Betty . . . especially Betty.

Laura dangled her feet off the bed, and felt around for her slippers. Over and over again, you'd have to tell her she was out, and she'd still argue. But an umpire couldn't allow herself, Laura thought with dignity, to be influenced by loud voices or jeering remarks. Justice was justice. The important thing, anyway, was that now she was umpire, the girls enjoyed playing punchball again, and nobody was sore at her anymore.

She slipped her feet into the slippers, stood up, and looked out of the screened window above her head. A real, wonderful, gray, miserable day. A day to stay inside quietly and comfortably. How boring sunny days could be when they went on and on for weeks at a stretch!

"Let's play checkers later," Laura said to Anne as they were pulling on their galoshes. Checkers was a game she enjoyed very much but there had been little opportunity up until today to play.

"Fine," agreed Anne, "and I get black, OK?"

"OK."

Rainbooted and raincoated, the girls made their way out into the windy, wet world. All around them, other figures in raincoats and boots scurried and giggled their way through the rain.

The long dining room was warm and noisy as usual. They had hot oatmeal and cinnamon toast for breakfast that morning, and it all smelled so good. Why was it that food always tasted better on cold, wet days?

"Gertie, Gertie, if you're able
Take your elbows off the table
This is not a horse's stable,"

sang a table at the other end of the room. Someone had been guilty of eating with both elbows on the table. Laura glanced down at her own elbows, a respectable distance away from the table. That was one thing — Mama always insisted on good manners at mealtimes. She would just sink through the ground with shame if anybody ever sang that about her — in front of the whole camp too.

"Amy, Amy, if you're able
Take your elbows off the table
This is not a horse's stable."

Could that be *her* Amy? She glanced over at her sister's table and saw Amy with a distinctly guilty look on her face. Well! She'd just have to have a word with her later.

"KP this morning," Miss Susan remarked cheerfully after breakfast.

"Again!" cried the girls.

"Last week didn't count," explained Miss Susan. "Today's the day you usually have KP, so get going."

"This place is more like a prison than a camp," Lilly grumbled, as they made their way to the kitchen. "I never even dry the dishes when I'm home."

Mrs. Wilson, the cook, greeted the girls by

name. She had gotten to know them quite well during their week at hard labor.

"Betty," she said firmly, "you can scour the pots and pans over here by the sink where I can keep an eye on you." She distributed standard tasks to the other girls — sweeping the floors, clearing and washing the tables, peeling potatoes, and helping the dishwashers with the dishes.

"I'm kind of pleased when your bunk gets assigned to KP," said Mrs. Wilson. "You've done it so often, I don't even have to tell you where everything is."

Because of the rain, the girls really did not mind as much as usual being assigned to KP. After all, there was no place special they had to rush off to on a day like this. Talking and laughing, they swept, scrubbed, peeled, and scoured with more care than usual, and had the tables set for lunch in record time.

"Well," said Mrs. Wilson, "it just goes to show that where there's a will, there's a way."

The girls smiled politely, and began heading for the door.

Mrs. Wilson looked thoughtful. "You

know," she began, "I was going to make baked apples for supper but..."

The girls waited impatiently. There was nothing in the prospect of baked apples to stir up any other kind of emotion.

"But," continued Mrs. Wilson, "with a little help I suppose I just might consider making apple pies. There's something about a rainy day that always makes me feel like baking. How about the rest of you?"

There were no dissenting voices, and, in a little while, nearly all of them were seated around the long wooden work table in the kitchen peeling and slicing mountains of apples. A few girls brought wood from the adjoining shed to get a good fire going in the big wood stove that Mrs. Wilson used to do all her cooking and baking.

Mrs. Wilson's arms and apron were soon covered with flour as she rolled out one pie crust after another. Soon a long row of pie pans stood ready for filling. The girls found it impossible to keep up with her but Mrs. Wilson didn't seem to be in any special hurry today. She laughed and chatted as she worked, her hands moving continually. Into the pie crusts went the apple slices. Mrs. Wilson hovered over each one, adding spices and dabs of butter before sealing them up and popping them into the oven.

The smell of cinnamon took Laura by surprise. She stopped peeling for a moment, and looked around. Outside the rain was streaming down, and through the kitchen windows you could see the branches of the trees bending in the strong wind. Here in the busy, bright kitchen it was warm and dry, and the smell of cinnamon was everywhere. To Laura, cinnamon meant good things to eat, which really meant Mama. Nobody could bake like Mama — not Mrs. Wilson — not anybody. Rice puddings so creamy and fluffy (they never tasted right when somebody else made them), with cinnamon; tiny little horns stuffed with raisins, nuts, and cinnamon; nut cakes, crumb cakes, apple pies — all with cinnamon.

It won't be long now, she told herself as she felt the familiar ache inside. Another few weeks and the summer would be over, and Mama would come home. Home would really be home again. She smiled as she began peeling apples. This was the wrong kitchen but still it was a cozy, happy place. Maybe the pies wouldn't be as good as Mama's but they would be apple pies.

The morning passed so quickly that it seemed as if no sooner had they finished KP than it was time for lunch. Laura was famished. She had seconds on the vegetable soup, ate every crumb of her cheese sandwich, and wondered approvingly when Mrs. Wilson had had time to make chocolate pudding for dessert.

The rain was still coming down steadily as they made their way back to their bunks after lunch. Everybody had to stay on her bed for half an hour whether she fell asleep or not. Most of the girls in camp considered this a ridiculous ruling. After all — who napped anyway? Only babies!

But on certain days there might be a redeeming feature to rest time.

"Helen got a package this morning," reported Anne, on the way back to their bunk.

"Really!" replied Laura with interest.

"From her grandmother," Anne continued.

"Oh, that's good. Was it . . . ?"

"Uh, huh," said Anne, "I saw it."

"Well — what kind?"

"Lollipops. A dozen."

"Mmm."

Candy was not really allowed in the

bunks. Girls who received packages of sweets were supposed to turn them over to their counselors, who doled out the contents after supper. But Miss Susan was one of those counselors who had a reputation for being a good sport. This meant, among other things, that she allowed the girls in her bunk to talk quietly during rest time and after taps, didn't fuss if they left some food on their plates at mealtime, and never inquired into the contents of boxes received by campers.

The girls lay down obediently on their beds, and waited until Miss Susan disappeared into her little cubicle. Then everybody sat up on her bed and looked over toward Helen. Nobody said anything. They just sat and waited.

Helen yawned loudly, turned over on her stomach, and made snoring noises. The other girls smiled at each other and shook their heads. Helen continued making snoring noises, only louder this time. Somebody giggled. Then Florence quietly got down from her bed, very slowly tiptoed over to Helen's bed, and sat down right on top of her.

"Uff," said Helen, and everybody giggled.

"Girls!" came a warning voice from Miss Susan's room.

Florence stood up, and looked down at Helen, who still lay on her stomach, making snoring noises, but her shoulders were shaking. Florence thought for a moment, and then began tickling Helen's neck.

"Rff," said Helen, and sat up on her bed. Everybody waved at her.

"How did you all find out so fast?" she grinned.

"A little birdie told us," Betty said.

Helen shrugged her shoulders, and got off the bed. She pulled a small box out from underneath the mattress, opened it, selected a red lollipop, and passed it to Florence. After Florence had picked a yellow lolly, she passed it to the girl next to her. It made the rounds of the entire bunk, and returned to Helen with two lollipops left.

"You can have those for yourself," Florence decreed.

"Gee — thanks!" said Helen.

Laura lay on her back, sucking a lemon lolly, and looking at the crisscross beams above her. How many girls, she wondered, had lain here on this bed, looking up into those beams? Had there ever been a girl her own age, a girl who looked like her, a girl who might even have had a mother who was in the hospital? Whoever had lain here last summer was a year older now, and in some other place. If there had been a girl here ten years ago, she would now be a woman, maybe married, maybe with a baby. Did those other girls in other years who had lain on this bed remember?

"Well," said Anne to the others, "it's my turn now. How can you change a pumpkin into another vegetable?"

Nobody knew.

"Throw it up into the air," laughed Anne, "and it will come down squash."

"Oh!" groaned the others.

"Girls!" came the warning voice from Miss Susan's cubicle.

After rest, the girls donned their rain clothes and boots once more, and went out into the heavy rain. They splashed in the puddles and held their mouths open to catch the rain water. They were heading for the Rec Hall, where most of the camp would gather to spend this rainy afternoon. The Rec Hall was in the other half of the building that contained the dining room. It was a very large room with tables and chairs made out of tree trunks, Indian rugs on the floor, and a fireplace at either end. Some of the other bunks had already arrived, and the girls separated into pairs and groups. The games that nobody had had a chance to play all summer were brought out — checkers, Chinese checkers, bingo, dominoes, cards.

Laura played checkers all afternoon. First she played with Anne, and lost three games in a row.

"You're good," she said admiringly.

"I can even beat my cousin Joey," Anne reported. "He's thirteen, and he says I should learn chess. That's supposed to be harder."

Laura played the next game with Amy. She won it easily, and Amy looked sulky. In the middle of the second game, with Amy on her way to certain defeat, Laura delivered some advice.

"The trouble with the way you play is that you're not scientific. You don't plan your moves. You just move. That's why you're not a good player. Think before you move anything. Say to yourself, 'What good will this move do me?' Take your time. Don't rush."

Amy looked gloomy, but she paused before she made her next move, and surveyed the board. Suddenly she brightened. "Oh, I see a good one," she smiled.

"Well, don't let me know that, dopey," said Laura.

Amy made her move, and waited, a broad smile on her face. Laura proceeded to jump three of her men.

"But . . . but . . . you weren't supposed to do that," said the astonished Amy, the smile quickly vanishing from her face.

"You just weren't using your head again," said Laura kindly. "Look, I'll show you what you should have done."

But Amy rose from the table. "Never mind," she said haughtily, "I don't want to play anymore. I'm sick of checkers." And off she went.

Laura was still playing checkers when the dinner gong sounded. It was amazing how quickly the whole afternoon had flown. Why, she could have continued playing for another hour at least. One of the good features of playing a game over and over again was how much you learned. Just this afternoon, she had started to perfect a new approach toward opening the game — moving her men in a wedgelike formation instead of spreading them all over the board. She'd like to try that out on Anne and see how effective it was. Maybe after supper.

"Oh, I'm starving," moaned Anne as they entered the dining room, and were enveloped by the warm, rich smells floating out of the kitchen.

Laura sniffed the air. "Wonder what it is?" she said. "Well, we know what's for dessert, anyway."

They had beef stew, lettuce and tomato salad, and thick slices of bread. The rain beat down on the roof, and, through the sounds of eating and talking, Laura could hear it, and enjoy it — out there.

"Thank you, I'll have some more," she said, as Miss Susan asked who wanted seconds. As a matter of fact, everybody did except for Betty, who, compared to everybody else in the bunk, was a picky eater.

"Don't eat too much," cautioned Janet. "You know what's coming up." This was a sobering thought, and nobody asked for thirds.

At last it came. Laura lingered over her piece of pie. My, it was good. Sometimes apple pie tasted even better than chocolate cake. Not usually, of course, but today for instance it was the perfect dessert.

After supper, Laura played two more games with Anne, and lost both. That wedge formation would evidently need some more work. The dark day grew darker while she played, and soon it was impossible to see the board or the checkers. They put away the games then, and the counselors lit the two fireplaces for an indoor campfire.

"Old MacDonald had a farm
Ee-I-Ee-I-O"

The singing began. Laura and her bunkmates sat in a row on the floor. Their arms were around each others shoulders and they swayed back and forth with the singing.

"Seated one day at the organ,
I was weary and ill at ease,
And my fingers wandered idly
Over the noisy keys.

I do not know what I was playing,
Or what I was dreaming then;
But I struck one chord of music,
Like the sound of a great Amen."

"Such a sad, beautiful song," thought Laura. "The Lost Chord," it was called, and it told of a woman who had struck a wonderful note of music, and had never been able to do it again.

The singing grew soft and slightly melancholy. They sang "I'll Take You Home Again, Kathleen," "Silver Threads Among the Gold," "Flow Gently, Sweet Afton," "The Last Rose of Summer" — and then, everybody was hungry again.

There was no question about what they should have for refreshments that evening. Popcorn, of course, made at the fireplaces. After Laura had licked the last speck of buttery salt from her fingers, she felt so tired, she could hardly wait to get into her bed.

It had stopped raining outside. Low, dark clouds moved swiftly under a gray sky.

"I think it's breaking up," said Miss Susan.

There was a strong wind blowing, and Laura shivered, even under her warm jacket. Oh, bed would feel good tonight! Her teeth were chattering by the time she crept under the blankets, and lay shivering there, waiting for the warmth to come. Slowly, it began spreading.

"A man," said Rachel, "was locked in a room with a bed, a calendar, and a piano. How did he eat, drink, and get out of the room?"

Laura's toes felt cold, and she rubbed her feet together. The rest of her was beginning to warm up.

"Everybody knows that one," said Helen. "He ate the dates from the calendar, drank from the springs of the bed, and opened the door with the keys of the piano."

Laura smiled into her pillow. She was all warm now, and very sleepy. What a pleasant day this had been. Thank goodness for rain.

More Rain

Dear Aunt Minnie,

Thanks very much for the box of gumdrops. They're all gone by now — and the girls in my bunk say Thank You too.

I'm glad you're having a good time in Albany, and that you think the boys are very well behaved. It's so funny having first cousins that I've never even seen. When are you coming back to the Bronx? Will you be home before we will?

This is the second day of rain we've had since we arrived here. Yesterday

135

was the first day. Right now it's really pouring but I guess it should stop by tomorrow. Some of the girls are tired of being cooped up for two straight days but I don't mind. I've been playing a lot of checkers yesterday and today and have really improved my game.

Send my love to Aunt Sophie, Uncle Ralph, and the boys.

> Your affectionate niece,
> Laura

July 28

Dear Daddy,

How are you feeling? I am feeling fine. Please send me some socks. I asked you in my last letter but I guess you forgot. Now I really need them. It's been raining for three days now, and I don't have any dry socks. We only get our laundry back once a week, and remember I told you that they keep losing my socks. I only have two pairs that match now, and two others that don't match with holes in them. That is not enough. Hurry and send me about five or six more pairs.

Yesterday we had a square dance in the afternoon and drank apple cider and ate doughnuts. Today we are supposed to have a masquerade. I am coming dressed up like a pirate with a patch on one eye. My friend, Mary Ellen, is putting all her clothes on backward, and making a face for the back of her head. She is going to be Siamese Twins. It's a lot of fun but I am getting sick of all this rain. This is the third day without a stop. Most of the time there is nothing to do but play games in the Rec Hall or go to Arts and Crafts. The mosquitos are terrible. All I do is scratch.

I hope you are having a good time. Do you miss me? I miss you. Don't forget to send me some *SOCKS*.

Love and x x x x x x x x x x,

Amy

July 29

Dearest Mama,

I'm beginning to understand how Noah felt when it rained for forty days and forty nights. Of course this is only the fourth day of rain but it feels as if it's always rained and will go on raining forever and ever.

We found a family of field mice in our bunk this afternoon. I guess their home was flooded and they were happy to find a nice, dry spot. But they didn't stay long when they saw us.

Even though it was raining steadily today, it wasn't as cold and windy as it has been. Miss Susan suggested that we all go fishing. She goes fishing a lot, and says she thinks the best time to go is when it rains. First of all, you can find worms so much more easily. There's a spot down near the lake where we go. There were hundreds of them there today. What I don't like is putting the worm on the hook. I guess I feel sorry for the worm. After all, they have feelings too, even though they are so tiny.

Anyway, we sat on the pier in our raincoats and hats and fished for about half an hour. Some of the girls caught sunfish and Florence caught a catfish. But they were so tiny they threw them back. Only Helen caught a big fish. It was a perch. We cooked it over one of the indoor fireplaces when we got back, and everybody had a little taste. It was delicious.

I started reading *Matorni"s Vineyard* after we got back from fishing but it was so noisy in the Rec Hall, I just didn't get very far with it. Can you imagine — I haven't read a single one of my books since I came here. They all call me the bookworm, which is kind of silly when you realize that I never get to read. I mean it's true I am a bookworm in the city but here I'm not so it doesn't make sense being called a bookworm.

The reason it was so noisy in the Rec Hall today was because they were holding contests. Every afternoon since the second day it rained, we've had a special event to help pass away the time. Tuesday there was a square dance — I didn't care for that too much. You know how clumsy I am, Mama — and don't say I'm not!

Wednesday, there was a masquerade. That was really fun. I stuffed pillows inside my clothes, and came as the fat lady of the circus. Anne draped a sheet around her real tight, made a crown for her head, and wrapped Fred, the snake, around her shoulders. She was supposed to be Cleopatra. You know — Cleopatra killed herself by letting a snake bite her. Amy really looked cute. She was a pirate with a patch over one eye, one earring, and a toy dagger she carried between her teeth.

For the contests, they cleared all the furniture out of the way. There were relays, peanut-pushing contests (pushing the peanut across the room with your nose), musical chairs, and lots of others. I didn't win anything but Amy nearly won the who-can-talk-the-most-and-fastest contest. She was one of the finalists but a thirteen-year-old won so it wasn't really fair. You know how much Amy can talk — she should have won.

Mama — I'm getting so good at checkers! I can actually beat Anne now 50 percent of the time we play. The only reason I was able to improve my game so much was because of the rain. So I guess it's true that every cloud has a silver lining. But for the sake of my bunkmates, I certainly hope the rain stops. They are getting very restless.

There is one girl in particular, named Betty. She's the one I told you about who always cheats at punchball, and says everybody else is cheating. Ever since the rain started she spends all her time thinking up practical jokes to play on people. Yesterday, she hid Anne's album of movie stars, and Anne was practically in tears thinking that she'd lost it somewhere. Later when she found it under Mary's bed, somebody had drawn mustaches on all the actresses' faces — even Shirley Temple's. Of course, Betty denied having anything to do with it. I helped Anne erase the mustaches and the terrible thing is that you can still see a line on most of the faces. Hedy Lamarr's is the worst. That Betty really has a twisted mind. Anne tries to act as if she doesn't care, but she does.

Your loving daughter,
Laura

When the girls awoke the next morning, they found it was still raining for the fifth day in a row. It was all that they could do to get themselves dressed. Everybody felt damp and dispirited. The building smelled of wetness, their clothes were clammy — there wasn't a dry spot anywhere. And then to pull on boots for the millionth time, and go out into that pouring rain, seemed the final indignity. Nobody talked at all on the way to the mess hall. Just outside, Anne slipped and fell in the mud. She didn't hurt herself but when she stood up, her whole left side from her head to her toes was covered with mud. Betty burst out laughing.

"What's so funny?" demanded Anne.

"Oh, you should just see yourself," Betty snickered.

"Well, if it happened to you, I bet you wouldn't think it was so funny," Anne cried and stamped her foot. Betty kept right on laughing.

All through breakfast, Anne glared at Betty, and Betty made faces at Anne. Laura looked with concern at Anne's angry face, and felt her own anger expand inside her. Would it never end? Why should a girl like Betty always get away with playing jokes on people who never bothered her? Why should she be allowed to make fun of sweet girls like Anne who never did a mean thing to anybody? Why?

And then suddenly, a tantalizing scheme began to take shape in Laura's mind. She watched Betty crossing her eyes at Anne, and she smiled almost lovingly in her direction. Revenge was sweet.

"Come over here, Anne," she said to her friend after breakfast. "I have something I want to tell you."

She whispered long and earnestly into Anne's ear.

"Oh," said Anne at first, "I don't know."

"Why not?" whispered Laura. "It's only fair."

Anne thought for a moment. Then she smiled. Then she laughed out loud. "Oh, Laura," she said, "let's go!"

After they returned, the morning just dragged. Every time they looked at each other, they started to laugh. All during lunch, Anne kept leaning over and whispering in Laura's ear, "I can't wait, I just can't wait." On the way back to the bunk for rest, Anne sang "Old Man River" at the top of her lungs until Helen complained. Then she sang "The Lady in Red." Laura's face wore a contained, watchful smile, but Anne began giggling as soon as they entered the bunk. She giggled as she removed her shoes, giggled as she crept into her bed, and the girls could hear the giggles continuing after she had buried her face in her pillow.

"Oh, shut up!" Betty said crossly, climbing under her blankets. A horrible scream immediately followed, and Betty came leaping up out of bed, fleeing to the other side of the room, where she stood trembling, her eyes and mouth open as wide as they could go.

"Girls!" came Miss Susan's voice.

"What happened? What happened?" whispered the girls.

Laura was laughing. She was sitting up in her bed, her face red, her finger pointing at Betty, and laughing.

"Oh, oh, oh," she gasped.

Anne lay doubled over on her bed, struggling for breath.

Betty clenched her teeth. Back she marched to her bed, and pulled aside the blankets. There on the sheet slithered about twenty or thirty plump, muddy worms.

Before any of the other girls had a chance

to put all of the evidence together, Betty grabbed her pillow, and began swatting Laura. Quickly, Laura grabbed her own pillow, and swatted back. My, it felt good! She jumped up on her bed, and brandishing her pillow with both hands over her head, like an avenging angel, she swung away with all her might at Betty.

Somebody flung a pillow from across the room. Somebody else threw another pillow. In about two minutes flat, the entire bunk was filled with flying pillows, pajamas, socks, and shoes.

Anne leaped on Laura's bed, twirling her own pillow around wildly.

"Hey, you're hitting me," yelled Laura.

"Don't fire 'til you see the whites of their eyes," roared Mary, attempting to scale Laura's bed. A flying pillow whammed her in the mouth, and she collapsed on the floor, laughing.

Fresh reserves rushed up to storm Laura's bed from the other side. Joan threw a blanket over Anne, and dragged her from the pinnacle.

"Rachel, get off my foot!" yelled Lilly.

On the battle raged. Except for Laura and Betty, who thwacked away at each other exclusively, the other warriors aimed their blows at everyone and anyone.

"Give me liberty or give me death!" Anne cried from underneath the blanket.

"Somebody please sit on her," ordered Florence, waving Rachel's socks around in the air.

Laura had just landed a mighty whack on Betty's shoulders, and Rachel was dragging Helen across the floor by her ankle when Miss Susan's voice rose high above the din.

"GIRLS!"

All action froze. Laura's pillow hung limp in her hand. Rachel, still holding on to Helen's foot, stopped dead in her tracks. Anne lay motionless beneath the blanket.

"I just don't know what to say," gasped Miss Susan, surveying the battlefield, "I just don't know."

Laura held her head up, and cleared her throat. "It's my fault," she said, loud and clear. "I started the whole thing."

"You!" said Miss Susan.

Laura nodded briskly, and climbed down from the bed. "Yes, Miss Susan, it was my idea so don't blame anybody else. I put the worms in Betty's bed, and I am prepared to take the responsibility for what happened."

"You!" repeated Miss Susan.

"Yes, she did," whined Betty.

Anne came and stood near Laura, and looked straight at Miss Susan. "I did it too," she confessed, "not just Laura." The two culprits exchanged loyal glances and awaited the verdict.

"I didn't do anything to them," sniffed Betty.

"Oh, stop it, Betty," said Florence. "You had it coming to you." She looked approvingly at Laura. "Did you really think that up?"

Laura nodded.

Florence shook her head in admiration. She turned to Miss Susan, and said, "We're all to blame for the mess, though — not just Laura and Anne."

"That's right," Lilly added. "We all threw things around so don't only blame them."

"Well, yes," said Miss Susan severely, holding aloft two ravaged pillowcases, "that's very noble, but in the meantime, we have all these torn sheets and pillowcases to think about. What are we going to do about them?"

"If we all spend the afternoon mending them," Mary suggested, "don't you think we could fix everything?"

The girls looked hopefully at their counselor. Would there be another week at KP and latrine duty in store for them?

"I don't know," Miss Susan said doubtfully. She looked at Laura. "I just don't understand it, Laura. For such a quiet, serious girl you certainly manage to get involved in all sorts of scrapes. But this kind of stupid joke I never would have expected of you. The others, yes, but not you. Just look at this mess. I hope you're feeling sorry."

From behind Miss Susan, Laura could see Betty sticking out her teeth.

"No, Miss Susan," Laura said truthfully, "I don't feel sorry." She watched Betty crossing her eyes now, and sticking out her teeth at the same time, and a feeling of righteous contentment spread through her. Justice had been done.

"We won't do it again, though," Anne spoke quickly. "Will we, Laura?"

But Betty was now thumbing her nose, crossing her eyes, and sticking out her teeth, all at the same time, and Laura watched her in silent satisfaction.

Miss Susan sighed. "All right, then, we'll blame it on the rain. Come on now, let's collect everything and get some needles and thread. And Betty" — Miss Susan did not even turn around — "instead of making all those silly faces, why don't you get a clean sheet for your bed?"

After the mess had been cleaned up, the list of casualty items was considerable. Two pajama tops missing in action, two slippers for the left foot, three for the right, feathers from two pillows still floating, five torn pillowcases, three torn sheets, and rips in two blankets. Also, one scraped knee, four banged elbows, and one dislocated toe. The sleeve in Betty's bathrobe was also ripped, and so was Laura's pajama bottom.

"While we're at it," said Florence, "I split the seam in my jeans last week. I may as well try to get to that too."

It was discovered that there were other items in need of repair as well. Soon an impressive heap of torn, ripped, or holey articles lay on the floor. The girls surveyed it contentedly.

"We'll certainly be accomplishing something if we get all that done," said Anne.

"You know," Miss Susan said, "I've got an idea. None of the counselors could think up anything interesting to do this afternoon. But I wonder . . . Do you think the other campers would like to bring their sewing to the Rec Hall this afternoon for an old-fashioned sewing bee?"

July 31

Dear Mama,

How are you feeling? I am feeling fine.

Believe it or not it finally stopped raining today. There is mud all over the place but we went swimming and it was so good being outside again.

Yesterday it was still raining and everybody was miserable in the morning. But the afternoon was a lot of fun. Laura's bunk thought up the idea. Everybody brought things that were torn and needed to be fixed and we had a sewing bee. I brought my socks and Miss Jean showed me how to darn them. It looks like the way you do it but not so good. Believe me, Mama, it's a good thing we had a sewing bee because I really needed those socks. Besides, everybody felt good because we were doing something important for the camp too. I mended two kitchen towels, and one pillowcase besides my socks.

We had a spelling bee too while we sewed, and guess who won? You're right. It was Laura. For a prize, they gave her the sheet with the most holes to mend.

Lots of love and x x x x x x x x,

Amy

Ghosts

"We are the only bunk," said Miss Susan, "except for the eight-year-olds, who hasn't gone on an overnight hike."

The girls sat around their council fire and allowed this interesting piece of information to sink in.

"We've been so busy," mumbled Florence.

"Now I do think," Miss Susan continued, "and I've told you this before, there are other things in life besides punchball. There's no reason why we can't take one day off and have an overnight."

"Well," said Helen, "I guess if everybody else has done it, we should too."

"That's the spirit," Miss Susan said cheerfully, "and besides, I'm sure all of us will enjoy it very much."

"When will we go?" asked Laura. The prospect of an overnight pleased her, particularly since Amy's bunk had gone on two so far. They had slept out in pup tents, two in a tent, on top of Mt. Kinandoga.

"No time like the present," said Miss Susan. "We can go tomorrow."

"Will we go to Mt. Kinandoga?" asked Anne.

"We can," said Miss Susan carefully, "but I have another place in mind. I'd like to go to Snake Island."

"*Snake Island!*"

"That's right," said Miss Susan in a very determined voice, "Snake Island."

"But Snake Island is haunted," Lilly said. "Nobody ever goes there."

"Well, it's about time somebody did," said Miss Susan. "That's all nonsense about it being haunted. We all know there's no such thing as ghosts and I would like our bunk to be the one to show up all this superstitious foolishness. We'll go there, spend the night, and when the rest of camp sees us come back unharmed, other groups will start using it again. It's a beautiful island, and a crime that nobody goes there. I just can't understand how people allow themselves to be scared of something that doesn't even exist."

"But — the Story!" cried Anne.

"Well, yes," said Miss Susan, "it's a very nice story, and all that. But we're not even sure it's true. And even if it is, we certainly aren't going to believe in the ghost part of it."

The Story was a very special one to the girls at Camp Tiorati. They had heard it told a number of times since their arrival, and had felt delicious shivers run up and down their spines each time it was told. It was tantalizing knowing that once upon a time, close by, a high and beautiful romance — like Romeo and Juliet — had been enacted, and had come to a tragic end. The Story told of an Indian princess who had fallen in love with a brave from an enemy tribe. Their romance seemed hopeless. But one night, the brave had come silently and stolen away his love. He dreamed that in some distant place they could lead a happy life together. It was a dark, moonless night, and they hoped to paddle across Lake Tiorati undetected. Halfway across, the moon suddenly appeared, casting a brilliant light on the lake. They were seen and pursued. At Snake Island, the lovers were captured. Arrows from the pursuers' bows struck down the brave, and the poor loving princess drowned herself in the waters of Lake Tiorati before her tribesmen could reach her.

After that, it was reported from time to time that the ghosts of the two lovers were seen on Snake Island. Fishermen sometimes heard a woman wailing, and occasionally, strange, eerie lights had been seen. The last group from Camp Tiorati who had camped there, maybe nine or ten years ago, had been scared off in the middle of the night when one of the group had actually seen the brave emerging from the forest, pale and staggering, with an arrow still in his breast.

"Ridiculous," scoffed Miss Susan.

The more the girls thought about it, the better they liked the idea. Maybe one or two of them felt uneasy about the ghosts but for the most part they were a practical, level-headed group, not given to such fanciful imaginings. And besides, there would be eleven of them going — eleven big, strong girls, counting Miss Susan. A match, certainly, for two ghosts — and one of them wounded besides. And then just think what would happen when they returned to camp after spending a night on Snake Island. The praise, the admiration — why they would be real heroines just like in a story.

"Ooh," crooned Florence, "I can hardly wait."

"If we pack everything we need tonight," said Miss Susan, "we can leave early tomorrow morning, maybe at dawn, and paddle over to Snake Island and cook breakfast."

The council fire broke up immediately as everybody got to work. By bedtime, each girl had her own knapsack packed with canteen, eating implements, and clothing. A pile of ponchos, blankets, and rope lay waiting in one corner of the bunk. Mrs. Wilson had promised to have their food all packed and ready for them by dawn.

They lay in bed that night, talking about Snake Island.

"You know that skull they have in the Rec Hall?" said Betty.

"Uh huh."

Betty's voice lowered. "I heard that was found on Snake Island a few years ago."

"Well — what do you think?" Anne asked

breathlessly. "I mean, whose is it supposed to be? I mean, was it one of the ghosts?"

"No, no, not one of the ghosts!" Betty said impatiently. "They say it was a traveler who spent the night there fifty years ago."

There was a silence for a few minutes.

"I don't believe in ghosts," Helen said finally. "It's all a lot of baloney."

"Laura," Anne whispered, "Laura, do you believe in ghosts?"

"No," said Laura. But she found herself shivering at what Betty had just said. So she corrected herself. "At least, most of the time I don't."

It was still dark when they stowed all their gear into the three rowboats, and pushed off for Snake Island. All around them it was dark and motionless.

"Blup, blup," went the oars in the water.

Gradually, the sky grew rosy, and by the time they reached Snake Island the whole lake was aglow with colors. They pulled their boats onto the shore, and, laughing and chattering, sat on the beach to watch the new day as it came.

"I'm hungry," said Joan.

Laura, Anne, Lilly, and Florence went off in search of wood as the others unpacked the food. The slight chill in the air felt good — it made the prospect of a fire and a warm breakfast all the more inviting. There was no problem finding wood. Nobody had been on the island for so long that right inside the small grove of trees that surrounded the beach, they found more than they needed.

A fire blazing on the beach, the sun shining now in a blue sky, and across the lake, clearly visible, their own home base — Camp Tiorati.

"They're still sleeping over there," Lilly said. The thought that only they were awake in a sleeping world made them feel kind of powerful.

"We should do this again," said Helen contentedly, as she held out her plate for seconds on eggs.

"You see?" said Miss Susan. "I knew you'd have a good time."

Although some of the girls had been on overnights before, most of them had not. Miss Susan had gone camping a few times, but still needed to check in her camping manual for some of the more elaborate details.

"First of all," she said, "we ought to pitch our tents. We'll need thick, forked branches for supports, like this." They all studied the picture in the camping manual. Two forked branches, supporting a pole, over which was flung a poncho. The corners of the poncho were held down with stakes. What could be simpler! The group trooped off into the underbrush.

"Miss Susan — what do you do if the branches aren't the same size?"

"Miss Susan — I can't get mine to stand up."

"Miss Susan — I found a lot of branches but none of them with forks."

"Miss Susan — Helen cut her foot with the ax. Where are the Band-Aids?"

They spent the whole morning pitching their tents. "Next time it will be easier," Miss Susan said soothingly. "You just needed a little experience."

Anne and Laura looked at their tent with pride. It was the first time either of them had ever pitched a tent or slept out overnight for that matter. There would be two girls to a tent, and naturally Anne and Laura would share this one. On hands and knees they crawled inside, rolled themselves up in their blankets, looked at each other, and laughed.

"Don't you wish it was night?" said Anne.

Laura sighed. "I didn't realize it would be so much fun," she said.

"Anybody want to go swimming before lunch?" asked Miss Susan.

Their dressing room was the grove of pines, sweet-smelling and thickly carpeted.

"Poison ivy!" shouted Betty.

Helen, who was wriggling into her bathing suit, leaped up into the air.

"There's no poison ivy here," Laura announced, looking over the ground professionally.

"Will you cut that out!" Helen grumbled to Betty. "You keep scaring the daylights out of me."

"Don't swim out too far," cautioned Miss Susan, after the girls had finished dressing. "I'm the only counselor here. And stay with your buddy."

All of the girls except for Laura and Betty were good swimmers. Anne, Lilly, and Helen had even passed the Junior Life Saving Test, and could swim across the lake without tiring. Laura could float on her back for as long as five minutes before her legs started submerging. She could also do the dead man's float, and something resembling a dog paddle. Betty couldn't even do the dead man's float. Since neither of them could go very far, Laura and Betty were swimming buddies. Betty still wasn't talking to Laura but silently they stayed together while their more talented companions ventured out farther in pairs.

Miss Susan was trying to teach Laura the side stroke. "If you learn that," she said, "you can go on swimming almost indefinitely."

Laura tried, as she had tried for weeks now. She kicked as fast and as vigorously as she could, thrashed her arms around, making a lot of waves, and went under the water still kicking and thrashing. When she came up and cleared the water out of her eyes, nose, and mouth, Miss Susan was laughing. "Nobody can say you're not trying," she said.

Some of the other girls were doing aquatic acts like the ones they had seen at the World's Fair. They formed flowers, did stunts, dived under each other's legs, and swam in formation.

They could swim for as long as they liked today, said Miss Susan, since there were no other groups waiting to get in. They swam for a long time, and when they emerged, their lips were blue, their teeth were chattering, and they had goose pimples on their arms and legs.

After lunch, they explored the island. It was green and golden, with all the birds and flowers an island should have. There was nothing at all forbidding about it — nothing that seemed menacing — no trace of ghosts. Betty saw poison ivy everywhere but Laura found lobelias, Indian pipes, and wood asters.

"When you're along," Miss Susan said, "I don't even bother bringing my book on wild flowers anymore."

They found blackberry bushes, heavy with fruit. The girls ate as many berries as they could, and then, with hands, legs, and mouths stained with blackberry juice, they were all set to go swimming again.

They swam all afternoon. If they felt chilly in the water, they came out shivering and sat in the sunshine until they were hot. Then back they went into the water until they felt chilly again. Laura didn't know when a day had passed so quickly.

For supper, each girl made her own kabob.

On a green stick, she strung any of a number of possibilities. Laura first put a piece of meat on her stick, then a piece of tomato, some green pepper, a small onion, a piece of mushroom, and then started all over again. The sticks were then grilled over the fire, and the odors were overpowering.

There just was not enough food that night. Laura and most of the others had to supplement their supper with peanut butter sandwiches. Later on, Miss Susan promised, when it grew real dark, they could toast marshmallows over the fire.

They watched the sun go down, igniting the sky and lake again as it had at daybreak. Darkness settled around them. No longer could they see Camp Tiorati across the lake. The night sounds filled the air — crickets, bobwhites. They drew closer together.

The fire blazed high in the darkness. How much brighter a fire seems at night than during the day. They toasted marshmallows. Laura liked hers brown and full of cinders on the outside and gooey inside. Anne liked hers lightly toasted all around. The night deepened. Miss Susan had a book of the heavens with her, and they held it open in front of the fire, and tried to identify the constellations. Everybody knew the Big Dipper and the Milky Way. It was exciting to figure out where the North Star was.

" 'Follow the curve of the Big Dipper's handle,' " read Miss Susan, " 'and you will come to Arcturus. See story below.' All right," she announced to the group, "see if you can find Arcturus, and I'll read you the story about it."

They found Arcturus, or at least they thought they did, and Miss Susan began telling them the Indian story about White Hawk and the Star Maidens.

Laura was just about to pop a nicely toasted marshmallow into her mouth, and Miss Susan had just arrived at the part of the story where White Hawk captures the most beautiful of the Star Maidens for his wife, when it happened.

A horrible scream echoed across the lake. Not just an ordinary scream but a crazy, laughing, hysterical scream. The kind Mr. Rochester's insane wife makes in the movie *Jane Eyre*. Miss Susan did not finish her sentence about White Hawk. Laura's marshmallow paused en route to her mouth. Nobody moved.

164

Again the scream came, louder and closer this time. A low moan broke from the group around the fire, and in that moment, just before they could get to their feet and tear off to the boats, Laura calmly put the marshmallow into her mouth.

". . . oons," she seemed to say.

Her calm arrested the panic. Everybody stared at Laura. "What . . . what . . . did you say?" asked Miss Susan, her voice pitched much higher than usual.

Laura managed to swallow her marshmallow. "Loons," she explained, "you know — loons — those birds we've seen flying over the lake."

Nobody knew.

"Loons," Laura said again. "They make a funny noise, like a crazy laugh. I never heard one before but that's what the book said."

While she was talking, it came again, a little further off this time. "You see," Laura explained, "it's flying away now."

Miss Susan began laughing. One by one the others joined in. "Oh, that's a good one," Florence roared. "Boy, did that have us scared for a while."

"I thought it was . . . it was . . ." gasped Helen.

"So did we all," laughed Lilly.

"It's a good thing we've got you along, Laura," said Mary.

"What book was that in?" asked Helen respectfully.

Again came the screaming laughter. It sounded as though it was all around them now. Nobody spoke for a moment.

Anne shuddered. "Are you sure, though?" she said. "Are you sure, Laura?"

"Sure I'm sure," Laura said.

"But," Anne continued, "you didn't *see* a loon."

"Well, what else could it be?" said Laura.

The girls drew closer together. Miss Susan threw some more wood on the fire. The darkness around seemed full of strange sounds.

"Shall I finish the story?" suggested Miss Susan, her voice still not quite normal. She began reading again.

"What was that?" screamed Betty.

"Oh," Miss Susan laughed a quavering, little laugh. "Probably a chipmunk . . . or something."

"Probably," said Laura. She looked around at her bunkmates. Most of them had their heads cocked to one side as if they were listening for something. All of them had a tight, uneasy look. Even Miss Susan seemed to have forgotten about the story of White Hawk and the Star Maidens. She was gazing off into the darkness, a troubled look on her face.

"Have some more marshmallows, everybody," Laura urged. She felt full of tenderness for them, the way she felt when Amy sometimes woke up at night frightened by a bad dream.

"It really was a loon," she announced with certainty. "I *know* it was a loon."

Everybody took another marshmallow, and Miss Susan finished her story.

"I guess we should get to bed now," said Miss Susan weakly, after the story was finished and the marshmallows had disappeared.

"Oh, I couldn't sleep a wink tonight," groaned Anne. "I just couldn't!"

"Neither could I!"

"I can't!"

"Me neither!"

"Sure you can," said Laura, getting to her feet. "Come on, let's go! I'm so tired I can hardly move."

It was amazing how quickly all of them fell asleep. First, you could hear lots of moving and talking in each tent, then occasional whispers and giggles, and finally nothing at all. Only Laura lay rolled up in her blanket, fully awake for a long, long time, her eyes open, her ears alert to every passing sound.

"Was it really a loon?" she wondered.

When the girls returned early the following morning before breakfast, they received a hero's welcome. In the weeks that followed, Snake Island became practically a thoroughfare, and every day some group or other could be found picnicking, blackberry picking, or camping out at night. Nobody reported seeing or hearing any ghosts, but then nobody saw or heard any loons either.

Laura and her bunkmates went on one other overnight that summer — to Mt. Kinandoga.

The Nightingale

Anne ran the comb once more through
Laura's hair, fastened a barrette on one
side, stepped back, and looked.

"No," she said, "that's not right either."

She removed the barrette, and began
combing again. "When a person has a long
face," she lectured, "a side part is best.
Here, hold this." She handed Laura the barrette. "But you have a long, full face so
maybe it would be better without any part
at all."

"My mother says I look best with bangs
and a part in the middle," Laura repeated
loyally.

"Mothers!" said Anne. She combed

Laura's hair back from her face, fastened the barrette on top of her head, stepped back, and looked again.

"Stand up!" she ordered.

Laura stood up, holding her belly in, and tried to create a pleasant, casual look on her face without actually smiling.

"Turn around!" commanded Anne. "I want to see it from the back."

Laura turned.

"Now sideways!"

Laura edged sideways.

"OK. Now go look!"

Laura licked her braces expectantly, and walked to the little mirror that hung on one wall of the bunkhouse. She was wearing her prettiest pair of shorts — the blue ones — and her brightest polo shirt with the red and blue stripes. Hopefully, she examined her reflection. She moved a little closer to the mirror. After a while, she moved back.

"Well?" said Anne, coming up behind her.

"It's very nice," Laura said, and tried not to sound disappointed.

"It makes you look more mature," said Anne. "Don't you think?"

"Ye-e-s," said Laura, "but . . ."

"But what?"

"Well — don't you think it makes my teeth more noticeable?"

"No," insisted Anne. "I think it makes them less noticeable."

Laura looked again, squinting a little this time.

"You see," said Anne, fluffing the ends of Laura's hair with her hands, "if you had a permanent, there would be more fullness down here." She removed her hands, and Laura's hair collapsed into its familiar, limp state. "But anyway, this hair style draws attention to your forehead instead of the lower part of your face."

"Really?" Laura cocked her head on one side, and moved a little closer to the mirror.

"You have a very high forehead — like Merle Oberon."

"Really?"

"And your eyes have a little slant to them. You know, the Dragon Lady in *Terry and the Pirates* wears her hair something like this."

"I know," Laura murmured. She had admired the Dragon Lady immensely ever since she made her first wicked appearance in the famous comic strip.

"You look sort of glamorous this way."

"Where's Laura?" Amy shouted from outside. She walked through the door, singing, "Happy birthday to you, happy birthday to you, happy birthday, dear Laura, happy birthday to you."

Laura turned, smiling at her, and noted the large package in her hand.

Amy stopped and stared. "What did you do to your hair?" she asked.

"Do you like it?" said Laura, smiling out of one side of her mouth.

"No," said Amy, "you look stupid."

"She does not," Anne cried. "You're just used to her the other way."

"Maybe," Amy agreed, "but she still looks stupid this way. Why did you have to change it?"

"Because it's her birthday," Anne said peevishly, "and I wanted her to look nice."

"Well, she doesn't," Amy continued. "She looks stupid."

"You said that already," Anne snapped. "Cut it out."

"I can't help it," said Amy. "It's the truth. If she looks stupid, she looks stupid, and she does look stupid."

Laura turned, and examined her reflection again. Amy was right — she did look stupid. Even with her pretty outfit, and the cuffs of her socks turned up, she looked no better than usual. In fact, the glamorous hairdo made her look worse. She unfastened the barrette, held out her hand for the comb, and firmly combed her hair back into its usual style of bangs and middle-part.

"Here," said Amy, "here's your present." She handed Laura a huge box. "And here's a card I made for you too."

Laura looked at the card first. On the outside was a crayon drawing of a girl wearing an old-fashioned dress with lots of lace and ruffles. The girl had brown hair and brown eyes, and under her was an arrow, pointing up, which said, "This Is You." Above the picture was printed "HAPPY BIRTHDAY," each letter in a different color.

Inside it said:

ON LAURA'S BIRTHDAY
by Amy Louise Stern

Although we often yell and fight
I think of you both day and night
And want to tell you here and now
That as a sister, you're a WOW.

HAPPY BIRTHDAY

Your loving sister,
Amy

The package was enormous. Laura removed a large sheet of newspaper. Inside was a box. She opened that and found the present still wrapped in more paper. Under that was another box. Laura kept finding more boxes and more paper as the present dwindled in size, and Amy lay doubled up in laughter on Laura's bed. Finally, in a very small box, Laura found something rolled up on a leaf. When she unrolled it, there lay her present. On a small piece of wood, Amy had glued macaroni letters L-A-U-R-A. She had shellacked the whole thing, and attached a safety pin to the back so that Laura could wear it.

"It's wonderful," said Laura, kissing Amy. "I always wanted a pin like this."

She pinned it on her shirt, and the excitement of having a birthday bubbled inside her. Just think — she was twelve years old, 144 months, 4,383 days, counting three leap years. Next year, she would actually be a teenager.

As she had expected, a package arrived for her in the mail that morning. The girls crowded around.

"Go ahead, open it!" commanded Joan.

"Maybe it's candy," Mary said hopefully.

Laura shook it. Nothing jiggled. "It's not candy," she declared.

It was a book — *Andersen's Fairy Tales* — and on the inside cover, Mama had written, "To dearest Laura on her twelfth birthday, with all our love, Mother and Daddy."

Andersen's Fairy Tales! There was a time, a long way back, maybe a year or so at least, when this book had been Laura's favorite. This had been the book that, more than any other, she took from the library over and over again, and read many, many times. But not for a while. It reminded her as she held it in her hand that she had been a different person when Mama went into the hospital, and that Mama didn't know how much she had changed. She didn't know how tall she was, how she looked in braces, and that she hadn't read *Andersen's Fairy*

Tales in a long, long time. Her tears began to drop on the book in her hand.

"Aw, Laura," Anne said, putting an arm around her.

"Don't cry," Florence said, taking her hand.

"Listen, Laura," said Mary, "even if it's only a book, they meant well."

"We're going to have a party for you anyway," cooed Lilly. "It was supposed to be a secret but we bought some candy and hid it under your mattress."

"My mother," said Rachel, "never gets me anything decent for my birthday either. Last year, she bought me a brown bathrobe."

Laura began smiling. How sweet they all were! "I'm all right now," she explained. "I just felt a little homesick, that's all. The book is fine," she went on tenderly. "I love this book."

That being the case, the girls admired the book loyally. The illustrations excited a lot of attention.

"Look at this one," said Helen, pointing to a picture almost completely in blue of a delicate, beautiful girl with a long fish tail. "Who's she supposed to be?"

"Oh, that's the little mermaid," Laura explained. "It's my favorite story."

"Maybe we can read it out loud during rest," suggested Helen. "It looks good."

Miss Susan raised no objections as long as they kept their voices down. In between munching the Tootsie Rolls that had been smuggled into the bunk to celebrate Laura's birthday, they took turns reading out loud the story of "The Mermaid."

"It's such a wonderful story, isn't it?" Laura sighed, when it was finished. "So sad and so beautiful!"

But most of the girls objected to the ending. They felt that, after suffering so much, the mermaid should not have died. The fact that she would some time in the distant future gain an immortal soul did not seem sufficient recompense for all her sufferings on earth. They also were not enthusiastic about the prince marrying someone else. It just was not fair.

"I saw a movie like that," Anne said, in defense of the story, "with Margaret Sullivan. You know how she always dies in the movies, and in this one, her boyfriend marries her best friend."

"I didn't like that movie either," said Rachel.

In the days that followed, much to Miss Susan's surprise and pleasure, the girls continued to read stories from *Andersen's Fairy Tales* during rest, and sometimes even after taps. With two flashlights shining on the book, there was enough light to see the words in the darkness.

Opinions varied as to which was the best story. Some liked "The Snow Queen" the best, others preferred "The Tinder Box." Laura stubbornly championed "The Mermaid." But everybody liked "The Nightingale." Even Laura, fierce in her defense of "The Mermaid," had to admit that there was something special about "The Nightingale." And, at the end of the story, when the emperor wishes to reward the little nightingale for saving his life, and the nightingale replies:

"You have rewarded me. I brought the tears to your eyes the very first time I ever sang to you, and I shall never forget it! Those are the jewels that gladden the heart of a singer . . ."

a hard lump always rose up in Laura's throat, and her eyes grew wet.

So it was no wonder when the time came for the twelve-year-old bunk to present a play before the Saturday Night Campfire that "The Nightingale" was chosen. There would be five speaking parts — or rather, speaking and singing parts — the emperor, the kitchen maid, the gentleman-in-waiting, and the two nightingales, the real one and the artificial one. And, aside from these, there would be enough ladies and gentlemen of the court to provide parts for the whole bunk. In every way, it was a perfect play.

Laura wanted a behind-the-scenes role. Maybe she could be in charge of costumes or props — something along those lines. Once, in the fifth grade, she and all the other children who didn't have speaking parts had danced a gypsy dance at the end of a play. She had not enjoyed that at all. She still remembered how awkward and uncomfortable she felt with all those eyes upon her. Being in a play was even worse than reciting poems at birthday parties.

The casting ran along smoothly at first. Florence, who was the tallest girl and had the biggest voice, was the obvious choice for the emperor. Lilly wanted to be the kitchen maid, and Betty, who naturally loved funny parts, became the gentleman-in-waiting. The problems arose around the selection of the nightingales.

"Who sings?" inquired Miss Susan.

Nobody did, as it turned out, except for Florence, who was in the glee club at school. However, Florence had already been cast as the emperor, and didn't feel she was the nightingale type.

"Who whistles?" inquired Miss Susan next.

A few of the girls did. Mary could even do "Yankee Doodle" with such a full, rich tone that it almost sounded as if two people were whistling. But nobody sounded like a nightingale. The situation reached an impasse until Miss Susan discovered that the camp owned a whistle which when filled with water sounded like a bird warbling. Now then, who should play the real nightingale? Somebody small and delicate, of course. Well, Mary was not really small or delicate but she was shorter and slimmer than any of the other girls, and she did own, among her other bathing suits, a plain, gray one — the perfect costume for the real nightingale.

Now all that remained was the selection of the artificial nightingale. As far as the music here went, Miss Gladys, the counselor of the nine-year-olds, had a music box that played waltzes. During the play, whenever somebody wound up the artificial nightingale, Miss Susan, hidden in a shadow close by, would play the music box.

"This is the most glamorous part of all," said Miss Susan, and she looked straight at Laura. "I think you should have this part, Laura. After all, it is your book."

"Oh, no! Not me!" cried Laura, horrified.

"Why not?" smiled Miss Susan.

"I just couldn't," said Laura. "I'm not the type. I'm just not."

"Sure you are," said Miss Susan. "And besides — this is the easiest part in the whole play. You don't have to say anything. We just have to dress you up in a gorgeous costume to look like you're made of precious jewels, and all you have to do is stand there, and let somebody wind you up."

"That's right," said Anne, faithfully, "you should have this part. You'll wear the nicest costume."

"But I just can't," Laura cried.

"Sure you can," said everybody else.

"And besides," said Helen, "it will probably get so dark while we're giving the play that nobody will be able to see you anyway."

In spite of Laura's protestations, the group decided she would be perfect for the artificial nightingale. And so it was settled.

There were four days in which to practice and assemble costumes. Mrs. Wilson produced a brocaded tablecloth that would be perfect as a cape for the emperor. With a high gold crown on her head, red pajamas, and sandals, Florence looked imposing. She spoke her lines in a deep, dignified voice. The ladies and gentlemen of the court wore pajamas too, and the little kitchen maid also wore pajamas with patches on them.

But for Laura's costume the resources of the entire camp were gathered together. All the junk jewelry — bits and pieces of necklaces, earrings, bracelets, brooches that had been used in previous plays. All the spangled and glittering scarves and belts that could be borrowed from counselors. Anything and everything that gleamed.

"You are a gaudy, glittering bird," said Miss Susan. And Laura shuddered. She worried about it during the day and during the night. Why did this have to happen? Why? Everything was going along so well. Why did this have to spoil it all? How could she ever stand before the entire camp dressed in all those jewels and glittery things? How could she? She would be so clumsy everybody would laugh at her. She dwelt upon all her weak points — her teeth, her straight hair, her chunky figure. On the day before the play she decided to speak openly with Miss Susan.

Miss Susan was not at all understanding. "It's too late now," she said briskly. "Everybody gets stage fright before a play. You'll be all right."

When the night of the performance arrived, Laura's hands and teeth began chattering even before she was encased in her costume. The others had dressed quickly, and were now surrounding Laura, wrapping this belt around her waist, pushing that necklace over her head, screwing rhinestone earrings on her ears, pushing one of a number of glittering tiaras in her hair. Miss Susan put lipstick and eye makeup on all of them.

"Look at yourself in the mirror, Laura,"

urged Miss Susan. "You're really a sight for sore eyes. Come on, Florence, move over, and give someone else a chance."

She led Laura over to the mirror.

"A real, gaudy, glittering bird," laughed Miss Susan.

And she was just that — gaudy, glittering, and somehow gorgeous. Any movement she made, something sparkled. She raised her hand to her head — on every finger a ring glittered. Bracelets up and down both arms, gleaming necklaces, a shimmering rhinestone belt. Below that she could see nothing, but she knew that from top to toe no part had been left unadorned. Underneath all that sparkle, her chubbiness, her crooked teeth, her straight hair merged in one gleaming, wonderful image.

"I'm a gaudy, glittering bird," she repeated, smiling, and the light caught her braces so that they sparkled also. "Inside and out," she said.

"OK, OK! Let's go!" said Miss Susan, and Laura's teeth began chattering again.

But the performance was a smashing success. Everybody remembered their lines. Florence was imposing as the emperor; Betty wonderfully funny as the gentleman-in-waiting; Lilly gentle as the little kitchen maid; and Mary marvelously noble and good as the real nightingale.

"The emperor of Japan has sent your majesty a gift," said Betty in the play.

"Let the gift be brought in," rumbled Florence.

Into the circle of light from the shadows beyond, Laura was led, hidden underneath a sheet. When the sheet was removed, a general "Oooh" of admiration could be heard from all the audience. It was fine being admired but Laura's teeth and knees never stopped shaking throughout the entire performance. Nevertheless she remembered to stand motionless until someone wound the imaginary key in her side. Then she opened her mouth, and Miss Susan, off in the shadows, played the music box.

When the play ended the applause seemed endless. Again and again they were called back to bow in the flickering campfire light.

"You were wonderful! Just wonderful!" chortled Miss Susan. "I was so proud of all of you."

Laura's knees and teeth had finally stopped shaking. As far as she was concerned, tonight's performance was her swan song. Never again would she allow anybody to persuade her to take part in a play. It was just too exhausting.

But before climbing out of her finery, she took one last peek in the mirror. Yes, it was just like before. Maybe a little bedraggled but still strangely fascinating and glamorous. Nobody else was looking, so she arched her head to one side, narrowed her eyes, and threw out one hip, like the Dragon Lady. She drew an imaginary cigarette to her lips, and, with nobody close enough to hear, she spoke tenderly to the image in the mirror.

"It's me," she said, "Laura Edith Stern. It really is."

Friendship Ring

Suddenly there were water lilies blooming on the lake. Yesterday, on their way back from a hike to the abandoned iron mine, they had passed this very spot, and seen only the usual flat, saucerlike leaves floating on the water.

"It's almost as if they know today is our last day," thought Laura as she pushed her way down to the bank to look at them. How small and white and delicate they were — such a melancholy flower! Above them, bright red and blue dragonflies flew busily back and forth.

187

For the moment, Laura put aside the question that had been troubling her. She sat down on the bank and let her mind float lazily with the little water lilies on the lake.

"Poison ivy!" shrieked Betty.

Leaping to her feet, Laura swayed precariously above the water.

"Oops!" shouted Anne, catching her arm just in time.

"There she goes again," Laura thought resentfully. It never failed. Every time the group went off on a hike, and dropped its guard for a moment or two in admiration of some particularly lovely spot, Betty was sure to yell "Poison ivy!" It was insulting, that's what it was, insulting. As if in all this beautiful countryside, the only thing that really existed was poison ivy. Oh, how that girl annoyed her! Like nobody else — even more than Amy! Laura straightened herself up, and looked furiously over to where Betty was pointing: the usual innocent-looking group of leaves.

Laura's sense of justice was outraged. She could not leave this lovely spot without a final testimonial to its innocence. No trumpets blared. No banners waved. But with the crusader's sense of right, Laura issued forth. She lumbered over to the accused leaves, lay down on top of them, and rolled over and over and over.

"There!" she said, standing up, and looking into Betty's wide eyes. "There!" Then she picked a sprig of the leaves and shoved it over one ear. "There!"

The whole group started to laugh — Miss Susan louder than anybody else. They laughed so hard, they had to wrap their arms around their sides. Everybody laughed except Betty.

"It is so poison ivy!" she announced loftily, looking away from Laura since they still weren't talking to one another.

"That Laura!" chuckled Lilly. "What a character!"

Today was the last day of camp. Really and truly, the last day of camp. Yesterday a card had arrived from Daddy, saying:

August 27

Dear Laura,

I will meet you at the bus depot on Monday. Look for me. Make sure you pack everything and see that Amy remembers to bring back her galoshes.

Aunt Minnie came home two days ago, and sends her love. She is too busy getting things back into shape to write herself. Mama is feeling better and better. Today she sat up out of her bed for two hours. It won't be long now. I can hardly wait to see my two angels.

Lots of love,
Daddy

Well, she could hardly wait too.

Everybody was supposed to be all packed before suppertime. Laura and Anne hurried to the Arts and Crafts shop after lunch to finish the reed baskets they were working on.

"Do you think my father will like it?" Laura asked, looking doubtfully at her basket, which was not quite round and not quite square.

"Sure he will," said Anne. "They always like what you make for them."

"Do you think it's too big though?"

"Maybe," Anne admitted. "But it can be for something else instead of his cigars."

"Like what?"

Anne considered the basket. "How about for letters?"

"He has something for his letters."

"Well — what about his handkerchiefs?"

"Handkerchiefs? Do men put their handkerchiefs in baskets?"

"Why not? They can if they want to."

"No," Laura said. "I better give it to him for his cigars."

"Then give it to him for his cigars," Anne said agreeably. "It's better a little too big than a little too small."

"That's right."

The girls continued working in silence, putting the finishing touches on their baskets. Laura looked sideways at Anne, and wondered again if she should ask her. She had confided just about every other secret to her in the course of the summer. Why not this one? But if she did ask her, and Anne said no she wasn't, then both of them would feel badly. Forget about it, she advised herself.

"Well, I'm finished," Anne announced, holding her basket up. "What do you think? Does it look like a breadbasket?"

"It's just beautiful," said Laura, marveling at the way Anne's fingers had produced such a perfectly round, tightly woven basket. "It's as good as the ones in the store."

Miss Rosalie also admired it. "You certainly caught on fast, Anne," she said. She looked over Laura's shoulder at her basket, and patted her kindly on the shoulder. "Don't forget your other things, Laura," she said brightly.

Laura finished her basket, and collected all her other Arts and Crafts projects — the dark red woven belt for Mama, which she had dyed with red sumac berries, the chicken bone necklace for Aunt Minnie, two painted acorn necklaces for her friends in the city, a bookmark woven of beads for herself, and that clay pot, which she might as well give to Amy.

Next they stopped at the Nature Shack to pick up their nature scrapbooks.

"Laura," Miss Helen sighed, "I almost hate to let yours go. Nobody ever gathered so many different kinds of leaves." She handed the large book to Laura. "And you mounted them so beautifully. Here's yours, Anne," she said, handing the thinner book to Anne, and patting her kindly on the shoulder.

Laura also collected the fossil rock she

had found near the lake, four huge pine cones, seven small ones, and the three plaster of Paris leaf molds which she had made. Maybe Daddy could figure out some way of hanging them up on her bedroom wall.

When all the projects had been packed in her suitcase, Laura discovered she had no room for her clothes. The other girls in the bunk had the same problem. Rachel sat on her suitcase, and tried to snap the locks.

"Here, take this," Miss Susan said, passing out paper bags to everybody. "Come on, Rachel, get off your suitcase. You'll break it. You've got enough in there to fill the Empire State Building. I hope your mother appreciates it."

"My mother," said Rachel, climbing off the suitcase and accepting three paper bags, "throws everything out when I'm not looking."

They were packed, and ready for one last swim before supper. Laura floated lazily on her back, and thought maybe she ought to ask Florence — if she could find her alone. Florence would tell her the truth.

On the way back to their bunk, Anne stepped on a grasshopper. The girls laid him carefully on a leaf, and attempted artificial respiration. But all in vain. He died before their eyes.

"We'll have to give him a decent funeral," Laura said solemnly. "That criminal Anne can compose an appropriate funeral oration."

"Who, me?" said Anne.

"Yes, you," said Laura.

The grave was dug behind their bunk, and the little grasshopper, shrouded in a leaf, was laid to his final rest in it. Tiger lilies and black-eyed Susans banked the grave. Laura found a flat rock which she set up as a tombstone. On it, with a pen, she wrote:

Here lies Gus the Grasshopper.

Dead before his time.

The girls stood around, heads bowed, as Anne preached the funeral oration.

"My friends," she said, sounding a lot like President Roosevelt, "we are gathered here to pay our final respects to Gus the Grasshopper. He died an unnatural death — the victim of a careless foot."

But here Anne started laughing and was unable to finish her speech. Even after she had been tickled and sat on, she still could not continue.

There was more noise than usual in the dining room that night. Although Mrs. Wilson had poured her greatest talents into this final dinner — roast stuffed turkey, mashed potatoes, cranberry sauce, and blackberry pie — many of the girls were too excited to eat very much. Laura could barely finish what was on her plate — everything tasted the same. Tomorrow at this time she would be home, in the city, eating supper from the familiar blue willow plates in her own kitchen.

About a week remained, she supposed, before school began. Although there were so many things that had to be attended to once she arrived back in the city, she still hoped that she could spend most of that free time reading. Certainly she could finish *Matorni's Vineyard* in a week, and, if Amy didn't bother her, the other two books as well. And soon Mama would be home with them. How fast the summer had flown but now it felt as if tomorrow would never come.

There was to be a final campfire tonight for the whole camp. Until they heard the familiar sound of the tom-toms calling them to the campfire, the girls wandered around aimlessly, unable to settle down anywhere. Everything was packed and ready to go. On the hook next to her bed, Laura's pink dress hung in readiness for tomorrow. How pretty and dainty it looked to Laura. She'd worn nothing but shorts and jeans all summer. She could hardly wait to wear a dress again.

"Move over, Helen, I'm all squashed in here," complained Florence as the group settled themselves down around the fire. Laura and Anne sat together, as they always did.

"No," Laura decided, looking at Florence, "I can't ask her either."

The fire blazed up, and the whole group sang the camp song.

"Skin-a-ma-rink-a-dink-a-dink
Skin-a-ma-rink-a-do
Camp Tiorati we love you
Skin-a-ma-rink-a-dink-a-dink
Skin-a-ma-rink-a-do
Camp Tiorati — we'll be true.

We love you in the morning
And we love you in the night
We love you when we're far away
And you are out of sight

Oh — Skin-a-ma-rink-a-dink-a-dink
Skin-a-ma-rink-a-do
We'll be true!"

Miss Partridge stood before the fire and spoke to them. Tonight, she said, marked the end of their summer vacation. It had been a wonderful summer, and she only hoped all of them had enjoyed it as much as she had. The group cheered and applauded. They were returning to the city tomorrow, she continued, to resume their everyday life — to go back to school.

She hoped that this summer at Camp Tiorati had given them all something new to think about. She smiled at Laura when she said this. She would like to think that they were carrying back with them a sense of wonder at all things in nature both great and small. It was always there to find, she said, even in the city. One needed only to look. She would like to share with them now one of her favorite poems. It was a short one, she added quickly.

"To see the world in a grain of sand,
And a heaven in a wild flower;

Hold infinity in the palm of your hand,
    And eternity in an hour."

Then Miss Partridge came to the part of the evening's activities that most of the girls had been waiting for.

"Many of you have learned much this summer," she said, "and deserve to be honored. I am now going to ask the counselors to step forward and make awards to those campers who in their opinion merit them. First Miss Ruth, the waterfront counselor."

Miss Ruth stood in front of the campfire and handed out blue chevrons to the campers who had learned the most about swimming. Laura did not receive a blue chevron but most of the girls in her bunk did. Naturally, Anne received an orange chevron for Arts and Crafts, and much to her joy, Laura received a green one for Nature Appreciation. The chevrons were made of felt and could be sewed on a jacket sleeve.

After the presentation of awards, Miss Partridge spoke to them again. She wished them a happy, worthwhile year, and hoped that she would see most of them again next summer. More cheering and applauding from the group. She told them that it had been the custom at Camp Tiorati for the past nineteen years to preserve some of the ashes from the last campfire of the season. These ashes would be used next year at the opening campfire. In this way, the spirit of good fellowship could be passed along from one year to the next. The youngest child in the camp was always chosen to gather the ashes into a special ceremonial urn. She beckoned to a small figure.

Little Linda Beaumont stepped forward and stood next to Miss Partridge. She was in the eight-year-old bunk but it was generally believed that she was only six and a half. She was certainly the smallest child in her bunk, and had just begun to lose her baby teeth. She also claimed she was six and a half. Children under eight were not accepted at Camp Tiorati but since Linda's parents had left to visit relatives in British Columbia on the day camp began, no action had been taken by the camp authorities. Besides, Linda loved being in camp, and all the girls — particularly the eight-year-olds — enjoyed babying her.

"Isn't she darling?" cooed Helen.

"She's so cute!"

"What a sweetie-pie!"

"Look, somebody made curls in her hair."

"Look at that big pink bow."

"Isn't she sweet!"

Linda held a clay pot with Indian designs on it. As the fire began to die down, all the girls rose, as they always did, crossing their hands in front of them, and clasping the hands of the girls next to them. This would be their last friendship ring. Miss Partridge began singing, and everybody joined in.

"Should auld acquaintance be forgot,
    And never brought to mind?
Should auld acquaintance be forgot,
    And days of auld lang syne?"

The fire was reduced to glowing embers. With Miss Partridge's help, Linda scooped some of the ashes into the pot. The campfire was ended, and the girls trooped back to their bunks.

"I can't sleep," said Lilly, sitting up in her bed as the sounds of Miss Susan's footsteps crunched away into the distance.

"Me neither," said Helen, turning on her flashlight.

"What should we do?" asked Anne, turning on hers.

"Let's go scare the thirteens," suggested Betty, her flashlight glowing on her bed.

"Oh, I'm tired of doing that," complained Rachel. "Let's stay in for a change."

Laura cleared her throat but did not turn on her flashlight. It was now or never. She just could not go home without knowing. But she kept the flashlight off so that the girls could not see her face in case they said no.

"Girls!" she said.

"What?"

"Girls!" She took a deep breath. "I want to ask you all something, and I want you to tell me the truth. Don't be afraid of hurting my feelings. Just tell me the truth."

"What?"

"Maybe I shouldn't say anything to you since none of you ever did to me but I keep thinking about it and thinking about it."

"*What?*"

"I really decided just to go home, and not say anything but it's so hard not knowing."

"Look, Laura," Lilly shouted, "will you stop talking and tell us what you're talking about?"

"I want to know," Laura said, very clearly, "if I passed the initiation."

"Is that all?" said Rachel.

"That Laura," Lilly chuckled. "What a character!"

"Sure you passed it," said Anne. "Naturally, you did. Nobody said anything because nobody even thought about it."

"I didn't know," Laura said in a small, happy voice.

"It's supposed to be unanimous," Betty said suddenly. "And besides, the ceremony wasn't completed because she muffed everything, so ..."

"So what?" demanded Anne.

"And it is so unanimous," Florence stated, "isn't it?"

Nobody spoke.

"It's unanimous," agreed Lilly.

"And we can finish the initiation tonight," said Rachel. "That's what we can do tonight."

"I'm sleepy," said Betty, turning off her flashlight, and creaking down under her covers. "Don't bother me. I'm going to sleep."

"Never mind, Laura," Florence said. "I can do it. We don't need her."

"No, you can't do it," Betty grumbled, sitting up in her bed, and putting on the flashlight again. "You'll mess it up if you do."

She wrapped a blanket around herself, and climbed up on top of her orange crate. "I'll do it," she snapped, "but I'm still not really talking to her. OK, get her blindfolded and bring her over here, and somebody tell her not to go and get us all in trouble again like last time."

Anne and Joan pulled Laura out of bed, wrapped a scarf around her eyes, and pushed her forward.

"Greetings and salutations," Betty began in a sulky voice. "Welcome back to the Lair of the Bear. Because you have performed all the trials and tribulations with honor and courage, we have decided to grant you a place of honor among our ranks. Is it not so, sisters?"

"Yea, it is so," chanted the sisters.

"We weave a magic spell around you to render you victorious against your enemies. Are you prepared for the spell? You may speak."

"Yes," said Laura.

"Listen then," Betty went on, still sound-

ing sulky, "WATUNPAROUNDINJACKS-
ONVILLARATCAMEPUNKADIDDLED-
AYFORUPANDINANTOANFROWHYN-
EVERCANDYLICKALACKTOJUMPAD-
UMPAPINKAPLINKATUNDADUNDA-
DOODDAYISHAMEYOUBEAHUNTIN-
GGOTADAYTADA."

She took a deep breath. "Now, spell the spell!"

"What?" said Laura.

"Can't you understand English?" Betty said distinctly. "It's a spell, so spell it."

Laura smiled, and started stringing letters together. "R-O-P-Q-F-T-O-S-I-L-M..."

"That will do!" commanded Betty. "Kneel now, and be dubbed."

Laura knelt.

"Where's the ruler?" Betty whispered.

"It's packed," came the return whisper.

"Here, take this, Betty."

"In the name of the sacred, saintly, solemn sisterhood of the Lair of the Bear," Betty intoned, and whacked Laura hard on one shoulder, "I dub you a sister in good standing." She whacked Laura even harder on the other shoulder. "So stand, Sister in Good Standing, and receive the STAMP OF APPROVAL."

Laura rose, and Betty stamped on her foot.

"Ouch!" cried Laura.

"And now," Betty sounded cheerful again, "THE SEAT OF HONOR."

Many hands pushed Laura down on the floor, and everybody sat on her. After a while, Anne managed to pull the blindfold from her face.

"OK?" she asked.

"OK," returned Laura happily.

"What have we got to eat?" Mary asked. "We always have refreshments after an initiation."

But the bags were packed, and only memories of former feasts remained.

"I've got a stick of gum," Helen finally admitted. "But I'm saving it to chew on the bus tomorrow. Otherwise, I'll get carsick."

"Tomorrow we'll find you another stick of gum," said Anne. "Let's have it."

She divided it ten ways, and the girls sat on the floor, and chewed delicately, holding the tiny morsel in place with their tongues.

"My mother," Anne said, "is taking a day off from work tomorrow. She says we can have lunch in a Chinese restaurant."

Anne's mother was a saleslady in Macy's department store.

"I wrote my mother to make fried shrimp for supper tomorrow night," said Joan. "We didn't have it here at all."

"I hate shrimp," Rachel said. "I hope my mother makes lamb chops."

They chewed their tiny pieces of gum vigorously.

"My favorite is steak with fried onions, and baked potatoes with lots of butter. Ooh — I can't wait to be home," Lilly moaned.

"Stop talking about food!" Helen said. "I'm starving to death."

They chewed on. Laura's contentment was boundless. Tonight marked the end of the long, strange summer that had passed. Not only had she managed to survive it, but she had even passed the initiation, and been received honorably into the Lair of the Bear. Thank goodness she had asked. It really mattered. Tomorrow she was going home, and tonight she loved the whole world.

Lilly yawned. "Now, I'm sleepy," she said.

They climbed back into their beds, and one by one the flashlights went out.

"Good night," murmured Florence.

"Good night."

"Good night, Laura."

"Good night, Anne."

A pause.

"Good night, Betty," said Laura.

No answer.

"Good night, Laura," shouted many other voices.

"Good night."

Laura's Luck

The bus driver muttered loud enough for everybody to hear, and leaned on his horn.

"Ra-a-a-h! Ra-a-a-h!" blared the horn.

"Whats-a-matter-with-you," he shouted, leaning out of his window. "Come on, move!"

Laura gazed contentedly out of her window, and scratched the mosquito bites on her legs. The city looked so strange — so busy, so dirty, so noisy, so hot — and so wonderful. The houses seemed much higher than she had remembered. And then there were the people! So many people, and they all lived in her city.

"I'm home, I'm home," something sang inside her.

". . . so I think" — Betty was talking; she sat behind Laura and Anne — "we should all make a date to meet somewhere in the city."

"Fine," said Anne. "Where?"

"Well, most of the girls in our bunk," Betty continued, "live here in the Bronx except for Joan and Helen, who live in Brooklyn."

"Why don't we meet somewhere in between," shouted Florence, who was sitting in front of Laura, "like the Museum of Natural History?"

"That's a good idea," said Betty, turning to Joan. "Do you know where it is?"

"What do you think I am — a moron or something?" complained Joan. "Of course I know where the Museum of Natural History is."

Betty smiled. "Well, I know that people who live in Brooklyn aren't very bright so..."

Joan hit Betty on the head with her purse, Betty shrieked, and the girls agreed to meet in front of the museum at 11:30 on Columbus Day. They would bring lunch, and have a picnic in Central Park. If it rained, they could have lunch in the museum's cafeteria.

"I'll see you before that though," Laura said earnestly to Anne. "I'll ask my aunt but I'm sure you can come next Saturday."

"And if my mother's home that day, I won't have to bring Paula," Anne said.

Laura's dress had become rumpled on the trip. Because of the heat, it also felt damp and sticky. It was tight around the waist and too high above her knees. When she moved her arms, she could feel it tightening across her chest. Too bad — this dress was one of her favorites. Only last summer, just before her birthday, Mama had bought it for her. They had gone to Alexander's, and Mama had shown her all sorts of dresses for $2.99. But she'd suddenly seen this one on the rack for $4.98, and knew immediately this was the one she wanted.

"It's too much money," Mama said firmly.

"Please, Mama, I just love it."

"Look at this one, Laura," Mama urged. "It's pink too, and just as pretty. That one is too expensive. We can't afford to pay all that money for a little cotton dress."

Laura looked at the cheaper one. It was

not nearly as pretty. But if they couldn't afford the other one, well they just couldn't.

"All right, Mama," she said quietly, "should I try it on?"

Mama was looking at the expensive dress. "It doesn't even have a decent hem, and I don't care for this kind of sleeve."

Laura held her breath and waited.

"Size 12," Mama continued, "that's too small for you. And they don't have it in 14. I'm not going to buy a dress for one season."

Laura remained motionless.

"Just ridiculous to charge so much for a child's dress." She looked quickly at Laura. "Do you really like it that much?" she asked crossly.

"Oh yes," Laura breathed, "it's so . . . so . . ." But words simply could not describe the beauty of the dress.

Mama looked in her purse, wrinkled her forehead, and counted her money. "Go ahead and try it on, Laura," she said curtly. "I don't want to stand here all day."

The dress fit perfectly. It had tiny little white buttons up the front, a dainty piqué collar and cuffs, and a full skirt which hid her stomach. She felt almost graceful in it, and she twirled around in front of Mama.

"If you get a year's wear out of it, I'll be surprised," Mama said with an exasperated smile.

And Mama had been right. Now Amy would inherit it. She glanced across the aisle to where her sister sat, chattering away to her friend, Mary Ellen. Didn't that kid ever stop talking for a minute? Laura thought, shaking her head. She noted with disapproval that Amy's frizzy curls stood out wildly in all directions. "She needs a haircut, and I bet she hasn't washed her neck all summer." Well — she supposed she hadn't looked after Amy at camp as much as she should have, but now that they were back home, she'd take her in hand again.

Laura patted her own hair. It had grown to her shoulders, and hung limply there. Maybe, when Mama came home from the hospital, she would ask her about getting a permanent. Anne kept insisting she was too old for bangs and straight hair, and maybe she was right. It couldn't hurt to try — once anyway.

She ran her tongue carefully over her braces again, exploring that piece of wire in back that seemed loose. First thing, she'd have to see the dentist, and get it fixed.

Thinking about braces reminded her of Betty. Now wasn't it silly for them to carry on a grudge that way? After all, they wouldn't be seeing each other much after today so why not make up and go home friends? Even if Betty had played all those jokes on her, and made fun of her, hadn't she done her share too? Maybe she shouldn't have put those worms in Betty's bed. Maybe she should have laughed at everything the way most of the other girls did. Maybe Betty was feeling the same way she was feeling right now. Good old Betty!

Laura turned around in her seat, and smiled tenderly at Betty, who sat directly behind her. Betty stuck out her teeth.

Quickly Laura turned around again, and pressed her face to the window. "That louse, Betty!" Thank goodness, she wouldn't be seeing her after today.

The bus was in the Bronx now, and all the lovely familiarity of the scenes outside her window enveloped her, pushing out of her mind all thoughts of Betty. She was actually home — home to her city, her family, her house, her books! She squirmed deliciously in her seat.

"Laura!" said Anne very quietly. "Here,

Laura!" She put her album of movie stars on Laura's lap. "It's for you to keep."

"Oh, Anne!"

"I'm sorry," said Anne, "that you can see the mustache on Hedy Lamarr's face but, aside from that, it's a pretty nice album."

"It's a wonderful album," Laura cried. "Don't give it to me. You love it so much."

"No," insisted Anne, "I want you to have it. To remember me by," she added shyly.

Laura thought quickly. The weight of love that lay behind Anne's gift was overwhelming. Only one thing in her own possession could match it. Mama would understand and approve, she hoped.

She reached into the paper bag beside her. It lay right on top because she had planned on reading it almost as soon as she arrived home.

"Here, Anne," she said, and placed *Matorni's Vineyard* on her lap.

"Oh, Laura!"

The heat on the bus was growing oppressive, and the mosquito bites on Laura's leg itched more and more. She scratched away vigorously with one hand, and with the other flipped through the pages of her new album. Randolph Scott, Errol Flynn

— Anne had first shown her these pictures in the infirmary. Shirley Temple, Myrna Loy — the day after the initiation when nobody else talked to her, she and Anne had looked at these pages. Jackie Cooper, Norma Shearer, and Hedy Lamarr. Laura smiled when she saw the mustache on Hedy Lamarr's face. As long as she lived, she would never forget how delightful it had been putting worms in Betty's bed.

"Page 7," Anne said, looking up from *Matorni's Vineyard*. "You never got past page 7, did you?"

Laura shook her head.

"I remember," Anne continued, "when you were trying to read it in the Rec Hall during the rain. I noticed you were on page 7 then. And the day after we came back from Snake Island, you were on page 7. And then, that night, just before we raided the kitchen, you were still on page 7." She smiled at Laura. "You can borrow it any time you like," she said, "but I'm glad you gave it to me."

Laura scratched her legs vigorously, and felt very, very lucky. It would be worth going to camp for two summers just to make a friend like Anne.

There must have been mosquito bites all over her legs because she needed two hands to scratch now. The bus screeched around another corner, and the bus depot was in sight as Laura glanced down at her legs. All over them, she saw puffy, red blotches — not mosquito bites at all but something else — something she had never seen before.

"What is it?" she said out loud.

Anne looked down at her legs. "Golly," she said slowly, "I'm not sure but I think it's..."

"There's Daddy, there's Daddy!" shrieked Amy so loud that Laura leaped to her feet, crossed the aisle, and elbowed her way over to her sister's window. There was Daddy, waving and smiling such a big, comfortable smile, such a familiar, loving smile, that, for a while, Laura could think of nothing else. She was so busy waving, she forgot to scratch, and she did not hear Anne finish her sentence.

"... poison ivy."

About the Author
As a child, Marilyn Sachs decided that the only thing
better than reading a good book would be writing
one. But what do you write about? After growing up
in the Bronx, New York, attending Hunter College
in New York City, and working for ten years as a
children's librarian, Marilyn Sachs was ready to
write. Since then, she has become a respected and
prolific author of children's books.

   She and her family now live in San Francisco. Her
husband, Morris, is a sculptor, and her two children,
Anne and Paul, are college students.